TO MADELINE-
REALLY HOPE Y[...]
ADOPT A PET.
RIDE A BIKE.
SMILE.

www.thegreatchiweenie.com

andy +

GU

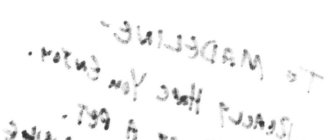

ISBN-13 978-0-9814900-0-7
ISBN-10 0-9814900-0-x

Cover Photo: Jayson Mellom, San Luis Obispo's *The Tribune.*

Caricature on Back Cover: David Brinton

Cover Design: Hannah Campbell

Adventures of the Great Chiweenie Logo Design: Casey Cordes and Cubby.

All other photos: Cubby and Megan.

WARNING: Riding a bicycle can be dangerous. Please wear all safety equipment and follow all the laws and regulations when riding a bicycle. Gu is safely harnessed into the backpack in which he rides, but is still at risk of injury due to any accidents or falls. Wear a helmet. PLEASE RIDE SAFE.

ADVENTURES OF THE GREAT CHIWEENIE

Biking Across America with a Pack of Teenagers

FIRST EDITION

by Gu and Cubby

The Great Chiweenie Productions
P.O. Box 669
Cambria, CA 93428
thegreatchiweenie@hotmail.com

Chapter 1

June 21ˢᵗ

Yes. Yes. Yes. Megan's letting me out. Megan's letting me out. Kisses for all. Ugh oh. Here comes the lady who talks on the speaker thingy. "Miss. You need to put your dog back in his carrier. He can't be out while on the plane. Thanks," she says.

"Sorry Gu," Megan says. No. No. Not back in the small place. I'm cute. Look at me, I'm cute. Look I'm too cute to be put back in there. Look, puppy eyes. Look. I'm holding my legs out, but Cub gently moves them into the soft-sided den. Drats.

I hate plane rides. Luckily, we should be getting somewhere soon. My owners, Megan and Cub, are here within my sight. The past two days, we have been crazy busy. Megan and Cub seemed preoccupied with all of the paperwork and logistics that still needed to be taken care of. A trip from one ocean across the country to another by bicycle is not an easy feat. Yesterday, they packed all of our bags and bikes for this trip we are leading over the next two months, hopefully we remembered all the things we will need. Two months, with seven youngsters, from one coast of the United States of America to the other coast. Megan, Cub and I will be in charge of the youngsters for a big chunk of the summer, hopefully motivating them through the depressing days while tagging along for the many happy ones. While I help out with the pups, Megan and Cub, my adopted parents, will take care of me.

I wasn't born in the United States. My life began in a busy town in a foreign country. A few of my family members weren't very nice to me. They would try to lure me over with food, just so they could get close enough to kick me or knock me down. So any time I saw food, I didn't know if it was going to be for me to eat or if it was just a trick. Not everyone there was bad though. One of my human brothers was my protector; he would feed me when no one was looking. Sometimes he would hide with me too. He wasn't treated very well either. When I saw most of my family I would still creep slowly toward them, hoping for a belly scratch, yummy food, or love. I was constantly hungry and usually sore. All that changed though, when my family came to the U.S. I wasn't allowed to stay with the family at their new den, so they sent me away.

It wasn't right away that things got better, but it was soon to come. Somewhere in a big city in the Central Valley of California, I was stuck in a chain link den with five or six others from different parts of California and beyond. Some had similar pasts like mine. Some had never had a home. We all hoped to survive this camp. Some of my roommates made it, but others didn't. Luckily for me, two humans came in and saved several of us from our cells. We were all so happy that our tails wagged until we were tired. We moved somewhere on the Central Coast, and our lives were better, but I still missed being able to sleep next to my human brother. I missed his gentle hands scratching my back as I slowly drifted to sleep. Everyday, many of us were taken for exercise around the ranch. I even got to play with one of my hairless friends who was lucky to be able to sleep inside of the house instead of the barn. It was too cold outside for them without any fur. I was fed daily and I was even taken to check on my health once, which I didn't like. Even though I didn't know it, my life was about to change again.

A funny looking male human and a happy female came to the ranch to check out my roommate. They were considering adopting him. I creeped out to say hi to the lady who saved me from my old cell and the male and female looked down at me. I didn't know them. I was cautious. They reached down to pick me up in their warm arms. After they both held me for a while,

3

they said, "We want him." I was adopted. It took time for me to be comfortable with Cub and Megan, but they are always great to me. It didn't take long for me to trust them like I trusted my human brother.

Cub and Megan had many great qualities. One of them is they truly love to bike. They messed with a hydration pack, one of those packs that have a hose to suck water with, three steel carabiners, and a harness for me. When those items were put all together, they could take me along with them on their bike rides without worrying about me falling out, because I can't. I even tried once. No luck. I just dangled with my paws in the air. With all of the distractions riding though, sometimes I have to let them know when I need food, water, or a quick bathroom break.

After they packed for this two month long bike trip, we went for a run at the closest beach and then headed to bed for the night. We did get a good night of sleep, or at least I did. Cub seemed super nervous with his unending energy and smiles; Megan was sending out her encouraging vibes trying to contain her energy supplies. Cub always gets nervous meeting new people, but once he can be his crazy and silly self he usually blends in with the pups. I kept my eye on Megan, because sometimes I need to protect her from things in the outside world. Strangers especially. This trip will be different for us. We all like to ride our bikes, but now we have to 7 teenagers to look after. They are from all over the country and beyond. How are we going to keep the pups motivated day after day? This should be interesting.

Earlier today, we met our first two pups. We took a ride

in a big gas guzzler with many seats and room to place all of our gear and more. As we headed to our plane ride, we stopped by a local small town and picked up our first pup. I was starving by then. I didn't get time to eat my breakfast before we took off and right when I saw our first pup, I smelled the rich cookies she was eating. Luckily, she was willing to share. Without a formal introduction, I gave her a name of my own, Yeah Food. She was quiet and had a hesitant smile on her face. She was obviously nervous, but was very nice. Megan kept talking to her the rest of the drive to our plane ride, and Yeah Food gave nice, short answers. Cub just sat there sipping his water so he wouldn't get sick while we were traveling.

We went through all the actions needed to get on a plane and we were scheduled perfectly to meet with another one of our pups at the gate before taking off. We approached the gate and spotted the new cub, looking bewildered as people walked by. He introduced himself immediately, which posed a small problem. Names are Cub's nemesis. He couldn't remember them no matter how hard he tried. This is partly due to his mind wandering constantly, but also his dismal hearing which leads to bad pronunciations. He likes to make up names for people and places. Unfortunately, he is usually the person who introduces me to everyone and everything. And, he talks a lot when excited.

Right after Cub heard the new pup's name, he immediately asked if he could just call him Frenchy, and Frenchy quickly with a slightly confused look on his face responded, "If I can call you Dumb American?". Cub agreed. Frenchy's talk was a little slow and was hard for me to understand, but his clean-cut polite manners were top-notch. Megan was surprised to see how quick Frenchy and I hit it off, but there was something about him. We got on the flight without any problems and I had to go into the soft-sided den.

Yes. Yes. I'm free. I'm free. Cub pulls me close to his face and I give him the kisses. Where's Megan? There she is as I push away from Cub to lunge towards her. Whoa. There's a lot of humans around. Humans walking every direction. Hugs on the left. Runners on the right. Yellers at the counter. Tons of them fighting for position around this long shiny looking treadmill. More kisses for Megan as she pulls me close. At least I'm safe with her.

Chapter 2

June 22ⁿᵈ

    I tap five times softly on Cub's face. I stare at his closed eyes. I gently press towards his face with both of my paws. His eyes open up and he giggles. "What do you want?", he asks as I perk up my ears. I'm sitting with my butt on Cub's leg and my back straight up into the air. Both of my front paws are held loosely against my body as I stare back, waiting for him to realize what I'm telling him. He likes it when I meerkat. "Do you have to go pottie?" Finally. I jump off and face the area away from all of the co-motion, and then look back to make sure Cub is coming.

    Last night and today have been filled with unknowns. Who else are we meeting? Will they be excited? Will they be ready? Yesterday Cub, Megan and I flew into this Coffee City with two of the young pups, Frenchy and Yeah Food, and quickly unpacked our bikes. We took a van to where we would stay the night and prepared for the arrival of the rest of the young pups. The first three pups came in to the airport right about the same time. I cruised on Megan's back, trying to avoid the uniformed people that felt I should still be in my traveling home. In the backpack, I sat on the bottom of the bag with just my head and front paws visible to the common Joe, Jose, Janet or Jezibel. Cub stayed on guard near our supplies. We met the first three pups, grabbed their bags and boxes, and headed to our meeting spot. Once there, Megan introduced everyone to Cub, which, as I've already said, is pretty useless. The process of collecting the pups at their gates only took a couple of hours with most of the pups arriving close to the same time, except for one.

While Cub went to wait for the last pup, Megan and I stayed around helping the rest of the pups unpack and rebuild their bikes. Some were faster than others, and some really didn't know what they were doing. I would go see how they were building their bikes and try to help them out, but then they would lose their focus. I suppose it doesn't make a difference, since I don't have an opposable thumb and all, but I know what to do at least. Checking out everyone during the afternoon, the names I made up were easily coming to me. One of the females put her bike together with ease, and wasn't afraid to get dirty in the process. She reached toward me as I was passing by, and I smelled her dirty hands and they stunk like bike grease. "AHHH!!!" I screamed as I ran away. Smelly Hands, as she would now be known, was bike smart and quite talkative, more so than the other pups surrounding her.

Everyone chatted, trying to get familiar with each other, but still getting their bikes put together. The first pup done building his bike was sitting against the wall eating some fancy dried meat product. It smelled like the cookies I get after taking medications, only better. I could smell it even though the bike grease was pretty strong. He built his bike with confidence and pride, and didn't seem to have a fear anywhere in his body. Walk and talk oozed out that confidence, and Alpha Jr. was his new name. Not old enough yet to lead this pack, but he has the personality to do so.

All of the pups finished putting their bikes together before Cub returned with a straggler behind him. Slow Poke dragged along, so Cub would slow his walk down to keep the pup in sight. Slow Poke was the biggest pup in every direction, and watching him as he built his bike with Cub's help was painstakingly slow. His talk was slow with a dragging of some of the sounds that made his accent unique. It was soon apparent that every thing about Slow Poke was slow. While they were building the bike, Megan tossed out the old savior of time, the hacky sack to entertain the others.

As I watched I noticed one of the females took off her shoes to kick around the small bag filled with stuffing. Nervously, I tried to get a closer view of the socks on the girl without getting stepped on. I dashed in, and finally got a feel when the sack was kicked over the wall. These were like Megan's Grandma socks, but fuzzier. I had to call her Socks. As I stood still, she would rub her sock up and down my back. Then I would have to run off before the sack returned.

While Yeah Food was still keeping her space, she did hang out near the other pups. There was another pup though, who wasn't even close to the pack. It almost looked like he wasn't even with our group. I wanted to go check on him, but he made me nervous. His hands waved back and forth toward me, a little quicker than I like. He seemed to be too cool for the rest of the pups, despite being the youngest in the pack by far. His long wavy hair was similar to Cub's at its longest, and he looked more than content sitting by himself. Cub and Megan at different times, tried to include him in the activities, but he always responded, "nah, not now." He continued, however, to wave his hands when I got near him.

Megan takes off running. Wait! Wait! I jump out of

Cub's hands and quickly catch up to Megan's heels. She continues to run towards this big bus waving her arms frantically. The bus stops. Whew. This is our ride to the campground for the night. She picks me up as she waves the pack towards us. Finally, I can take a nap on the bus.

Chapter 3

June 25th

Water is spraying off the tires up into my face. I'm trying to hide my face behind Cub's helmet, but the water is running off like the waterfalls on the side of this road. Everyone has all of their rain gear on - pants, jackets, and even things to protect all of their supplies. Don't they realize I only brought one coat for the whole trip? I'm getting soaked. I'm riding with Cub today. I wish he would just stop and hide under a tree or something till it stops raining. Today is gonna take forever! We're going very slow up this climb and this is only the first of the passes. Even though the days are the longest they can be, it's still chilly up on these mountains. I can even see snow on some of the Dish Soap Mountaintops.

I don't remember many thing about the two days before today except the road was flat and long. I felt like I was on the bike for a couple of weeks. All the pups obviously hadn't been riding much before the trip, because they were going slow while complaining about minute things. They definitely did not look comfortable on their bikes. The few people who looked comfortable, kept having bicycle problems. Alpha Jr. was having issues with the rack on his bike. He's a great rider with a positive aura about him, but he was frustrated because he kept having to adjust the bike so his heel wouldn't kick the bags on the bike. I thought the bags were called panty ears, but I'm not sure about that. Today seems like its been going better, though.

Other than the time sitting on the bike, sitting outside the grocery stores was taking just as long. Everyone would go in, except for Cub, and it seemed like they would never return. Finally they would come out with bags and bags of food. All of them would eat a bit, then they pack different things on different bikes. Stuff that can squash is put under the big pan on Smelly Hands bike. Megan stored most of those yucky veggie things, while Cub always got chocolate donuts that he wouldn't share with me. He also carried this big tin container that smelled like gas, that he only got out when we had to heat up the food. Each person packed a piece of the pie (mmm...pie sounds good right now). We did meet an interesting fellow that everyone called Cat Man outside of the store the first day of riding. Everyone compared Cat Man to us, but I couldn't see how a guy riding with

14

a cat on his head and shoulders even compares. He passed on some advice and was on his way.

So far today, Cub and I have been riding in the back of the pack, making sure everyone was okay. However, the group became so spread out that we rode in circles behind whoever was last. If we rode in a straight line, going that slow, I think the bike would tip over. Cub and I probably rode three times farther than everyone else, but I'm glad because I hate stopping. I just like the wind against my ears. Just sitting in the rain stinks. The smells on this road were amazing though. The trees all smell different. Water dropped off the rocks on to the side of the road. We even cruised by a beautiful lake that was happy to see the water dropping. Luckily, there weren't too many of the gas-fumed vehicles driving past us all day. People were scarce and so were the places to get food. We hadn't seen any place to get food since the pie heaven where we stopped to use the restroom. I think Cub started to worry about the rest of the day...he wasn't eating or drinking as much, and was handing the young pups food, water, or just positive words whenever he had a chance.

Here we are, regrouping just before we ascend this last part of the second pass. The rain has finally stopped, but everyone looks chilled to the bone. Whines and whimpers about the lack of food and water are flying around. The darkness is coming, we need to go. Megan said earlier we couldn't ride in the dark for safety reasons...lack of night vision I assume. We are supposed to climb this last pass then go down for a long way to the campground with food. Unless we can stop time, I can't see us making it that far before its pitch dark out here. Here we go. Back on the bike, grinding out these last couple of miles to the top.

Cub and I are at the top. We took the lead the last couple

of miles to hopefully motivate the others to keep up. It only took
an hour. Let's just say that I can see a couple thousand stars
above. I think this is the dark Megan said we couldn't ride in.
I'm searching in the forest for a place to lay my head. Ah...this
spot would be a great place to den up for the night.
"Gu...GU!!!" I hear Cub call out. I must have dozed off,
because everyone is here. They look beat.

It was just decided that we were going straight to bed and
would sleep in two tents, guys in one and girls in the other. First
thing in the morning, we would ride to the campground with food
down the hill...sounds easy enough. It's really cold. As I walk
around, I can feel ice patches under some of the tall giant trees.
Hopefully, all of the body heat will keep the den warm.

"What's that noise? What's that noise? What's that
noise?" I keep saying. We couldn't have been asleep for longer
than a cat nap, but I hear voices in the distance. I wake up
everyone in the two tents.

"Oooo...Oh lay oh lay!!" we all hear as this light starts to
appear on our dens. Whose shadows are those? They're getting
bigger!

Frenchy elbows Cub and says, "Go check what it is."
Cub says back, "No, we're okay in here."
"OOOO...OH LAY OH LAY!!" just got louder.

Megan says to Cub, *"Quit messing around...we're trying to sleep!"*

Cub responds with, *"It wasn't us."* As the shadows keep getting bigger, everyone covers their heads with their sleeping bag, each person breathing out of a little hole at the top. What are they scared of? I want to know what, or who is out there. Do they all think that by hiding like that that no one is going to see them? We probably smell worse than anything out in this forest.

Silence. The shadows disappear and we can't hear anyone. Cub finally unzips the den to check out what is going on. I go out with him. He says, *"what were you all scared of? There is nothing out here."*

"OOOO... OH LAY OH LAY!!!" screams out of the forest just as I see some lights in the distance. I start to say something. Cub grabs me and jumps into the tent faster than a I can bury a bone. Everyone is hiding again...panting so loud. Cub looks super nervous and seems to be getting ready to do something that he's not ready to do. He looks like he does before a technical downhill on a mountain bike section. I can hear everyone's heartbeats. They are almost as fast as mine. The heartbeats speed up even more. Our tent zipper is starting to move...the chants are right outside of our den.

18

The zipper is all the way open and Cub jumps up and screams, "oooooooohaahaaaaaaaaaa!!!!!" I don't know if that was supposed to be a word, but it wasn't. A light turns on. We all look up and see a little girl standing there.

She reaches out her hand and says, "Would you like to buy some girl scout cookies?".

"YEAH!" I call out, but no one seems to be listening to me.

"Get out of their tent," calls out a louder bigger woman, "you're not supposed to open their tents."

Food in everyone's belly, including mine, is a wonderful thing. All of the young Girl Scouts are sitting around listening to one of Cub's campfire stories as the adults talk to most of the pups. Luckily they were on their night hike or we would have never have been seen or fed. I think all of the food is gone now, so I'm going to bed.

Chapter 4

June 28th

"Get it off of me. Get it off of me", I tell the pups. They're not listening and it's driving me nuts. "Get it off, NOW!" The whole pack is just laughing it up. I don't speak up too often, but this is ridiculous. Why aren't they getting this dumb cowboy hat off of me? Just get it off. Oh, I see the light. Could it be? Yes, yes it is off for good. I can see the hat in Yeah Food's hands...she won't put it on me.

The past two days have gone off without any real problems. We were all still very thankful for the Girl Scout Fairies that visited our dens. I couldn't imagine what the next day would have been like if we didn't have that food. As a group we decided not to kill ourselves this early in the trip. Megan thought that if we hated riding this early that the next couple of months would seem like an eternity. Alpha Jr.'s bike problems were fixed. Frenchy was slowly starting to sound like the rest of the pack and a few of the youngsters were destined for puppy love.

The only ride we did this day was down the hill to enjoy the small town just off of the main drag. It was amazing to see all the frowns disappear with a little time off the bikes and some more cookies. The mountains around us were filled with pine trees with patches of shrubs and rocks. The town itself wasn't more than a general store with a café. There were a few other things, but the hot drinks were the packs' dream come true. The ride down and out of the mountains was my favorite part of the trip so far. Megan and I took off down the road. The trees flew by, almost unrecognizable at times, and tears of joy were building in my eyes (or maybe tears of pain from the bugs that got in there). My ears were perked and someone said I looked like a gremlin as we bombed the descent. I kept looking over Megan's shoulder to get a better view and to get more of the tantalizing smells in my snot stream. Since we were the leaders, no one was allowed to pass us as we tried to keep safe distances between each of us. We stopped at the bottom of the grade and Megan pulled out the camera to take some high speed shots. Each pup flew by with joy in their faces (possibly because we already decided just to do the downhill for the day). It was great.

It was interesting to see who hung out with each other

during our day of play. Slow Poke and Young Pup were always side-by-side and usually hunting for food of some sort. Alpha Jr. hung out with the ladies more than the fellas, but seemed comfortable wherever he settled his paws. The ladies seemed to stick together like sap on a tree. However, every once in awhile, Yeah Food would get some time to herself away from Smelly Hands and Socks. At times Yeah Food looked uncomfortable with the group, but I think the fake smile was turning more genuine. Frenchy on the other hand is what I call a sniffer...checking everyone out constantly, even Cub and Megan.

I rarely found time to myself, before someone needed my help for something. I'll get into something good, about ready to roll around and I hear "Gu...GU!". Foiled again. I did meet some interesting characters yesterday...one fella who just laid around at the store/coffee shop and looked very much like that famous fella on the side of all of those buses. He didn't say much till Cub accidentally stepped on him...he did speak his mind at that point, barking and yipping at Cub. The other fella, appeared to be his younger brother, was a little more talkative, even to the point where some people around would tell him to "settle down", or even just to "shut up". Both of the fellas were very cordial and wished us luck once we departed after our relaxing breakfast and hot drinks. Our day fixing bikes, hanging out, and getting to know each other had been a success.

The next day, a western style town that had horse-drawn carriages cruising up and down the main drag was our next stop. Lunch was tons of pizza topped off with some amazing smooth and extra creamy ice cream. The sun was starting to beat us up, so that ice cream was the treat of all treats. All the smells of people, horses, food, and gift shops were about to disappear. Before we left the outskirts of town, we met a nice three legged fella that didn't bark at all. He was dark and light, with a thick winter coat that didn't seem reasonable in the hot weather. He got around pretty well with his disability. The boy that was hanging out with him did enough talking for the both of them. He offered us water and was super friendly. The boy asked a lot of questions about our trip and the pack enjoyed answering him. The boy and the three-legged fella wished us luck, and we took off.

I rode with Megan again, for the day. I like riding with her, because its easy to make sure she is doing alright. When I'm with Cub, I sometimes have to move my body around in uncomfortable positions to see how she is doing and sometimes I won't see her for hours...it's tough. I worry lots during those times.

We weren't in the cool forests anymore. As we got miles away from the western-esque town, we started to see the drier side of this first state. I think we're still in the first state because I hadn't heard any news of a border crossing. It was still forested, but what a difference! Very little shade lined the roads and the temperature seemed to keep rising. The directions were easy through those parts, because we had pretty much been on the same road throughout. The sights and smells sure had changed. No more frogs. And no more cascading waterfalls. Big pick-up trucks dominated the roads. No more of the moving houses we saw earlier.

Megan seemed aggravated that some of the young pups

were not being totally safe. She kept mentioning these things she called rules. I don't know what they are, but I'm guessing I didn't need to follow them, being a dog and all. Young Pup keeps drafting off the others in the group, and Megan tells him over and over again not to. Usually, when I ride with Megan and Cub, we always draft off the person in front...that's the way of the biker. Birds do the same thing to save energy. It's easier to ride...period. Maybe the rules had something to do with the company that they are working for and possibly due to the risk of running into each other. Young Pup backed off and we struggled to maintain a good pace. The wind wasn't super strong, but it was blowing into our faces. We pushed through using way more energy than we needed to if the group would work together instead of being spaced out like we were. We couldn't have been going very fast. I couldn't see the speedometer from my position, but the dry fence posts were not going past as fast as the wetter trees had earlier.

Fence posts and bushes. Fence posts and bushes. Finally, it looked like we were leaving the fields of fence posts and would be heading back into the forest. We regrouped. Everyone sucked on their water and threw a few pieces of their favorite granola bar in their mouth. Cub was our navigator. "We have to head up Poop Poop Pass." The giggles flew. Apparently Poop

Poop Pass was our big barrier for the day and afterwards, the ride would cruise a little faster.

Poop Poop was easy for the pack, especially compared to the Dish Soap Mountains. The forest was different, but still alive with smells...warm smells. This time the downhills were safe and fast. Not a gas fumed vehicle could be seen. We left that forest again and headed on a road that pretty much paralleled a river. This area was quite different though. The trees for the moment were gone.

We shouldn't have to go much farther before we settle down for the night. I'm tired of sitting here. Are we done? Are we done? We're getting off. Whew. Hopefully dinner won't take long...I'm ready to curl up in a ball and sleep for the night.

Chapter 5

June 30th

Campgrounds, campgrounds...we don't need no stinking campgrounds. This is nice. The leftovers from dinner fill my belly as we all den up for the night. Mm mm....chicken. This is the best place we've stayed so far. Megan and Cub are talking right now to the woman who owns this abandoned building. She and her husband offered us the place to stay, because no one uses it. It's right beside the restaurant and store. The excitement is in the air...most of the pups haven't had the opportunity to sleep in a place like this before, out in the middle of what to most humans would call nowhere. Two separate buildings with miles of fields around them.

Over the past couple of days we had learned some key things that hopefully would help our pack for the rest of the journey. A nice man told us yesterday that people can camp in any city park, so last night we stayed at this cool park next to the river in a small town. We arrived late after our longest day in the saddle. We pulled in just as the sun was starting to set over the mountains in the distance. The light was just right. The grassy park with a small basketball court was perfect. Cub always carried a basketball with him. I hate the basketball. The loud thumps on the ground echo and radiate through me. The great thing about that place was that I could stay on the other side of the park with those who decided not to play. Frenchy, Slow Poke, Yeah Food and Alpha Jr. all shot hoops with Cub. They looked nice and relaxed. Yeah Food even looked relaxed with the males in the group, which was a first. Socks, Smelly Hands, and Young Pup hung out together with Megan. I think that Megan hung out with me to make me feel comfortable...she knows I hate The Ball. Young Pup was being rude to the girls, but kept following them around. His smile still creeped me out. I don't know why. Out of everyone, he was having the hardest time fitting in with the rest of the group right now.

We all went to sleep without the tents in the beautiful warm evening. I burrowed my way into the sleeping bag and slept superbly. When the sun came up, Cub and I got things ready for breakfast. I had the chance to eat before everyone else. Things had to get going quickly, because we were already a couple of days behind schedule. Apparently, the places where we pick up mail and our final arrival date controlled our trip. We had to get to preplanned post offices so Cub and Megan could get the mail for the group. This included the money for each week. The stress of getting miles in was already upon us, however, some of the rules were less stressed. Megan and Cub gave up on the idea of keeping the group from drafting, but did enforce the rules of the road which included staying as far to the right as possible. A few in the pack liked to ride side by side so they can have a good conversation, but were always told as soon as possible to get to the right. We didn't want any close calls with the gas powered vehicles.

The amazing older couple that ran the restaurant just went to their sleeping hole and everyone seemed grateful for the generosity the couple showed. Darkness is starting to set in and my eyes can't stay open. I'm trying to sit up and listen to the pack, but my eyes...

Chapter 6

July 4th

I'm hiding in Megan's sweatshirt. The fuzzy inner parts keep me warm, but also helps reduce the loud snaps, crackles, pops, and booms that are filling the night sky. We rode all day just so we could sit here in the field next to the lake and watch this miserable light and sound show humans call fireworks. I wish I had earplugs. One of these things is going to hit the group and our trip will be done for, I just know it. I feel like the pack when they were hiding from the girl scouts up in the mountains earlier in the trip with just a small breathing hole to keep me alive.

Three days ago, we finally drifted off the main road that we had been on most of the trip. We took the friendly advice from the restaurant owners to avoid the General's Pass and headed north for a shorter climb...Shorebird Pass. Alpha Jr. started an interesting topic of conversation that morning as we left. Jr. said "You know, if this was an area we knew, we wouldn't take advice from the strangers we've taken advice from. We probably wouldn't have ever talked to them." Now, some in the group disagreed, but others felt that this would more than likely be true. It was interesting and little did the pack realize, but the ride that morning was the quickest we had been on yet because the conversation diverted their attention.

Our beginning days sitting at the big grocery stores has switched to the days sitting at the small general store, restaurant, and pet store all in one. I'm never allowed in, but the time taken to get food was dramatically quicker at the smaller stores where I can see everyone in the store from the front window. Still, the discussions and sometimes arguments on the food selection continued. After lunch we had our first swimming hole experience. The sun had beat on us all morning, so this was a treat. I didn't want in, but was forced to stand up to my belly on the water's edge. I had to admit, it was cool and refreshing. I stood there as most of the pups splashed around. As the splashes started to get close to me, I made a run for it out of the water. I shook off and then I was so happy to be out of the water, I galloped around the others who were hanging around out of the water. Cub can't swim, so he just had his head up for safety issues and Young Pup was just wandering after his own short stint in the swimming hole.

The next two and a half days were tough for the pack...more mentally than physically. Tempers were short. Frustration due to flat tires, a long climb, confusion on where to sleep, and rain turned normal human conversation to short excessive barking at each other. The positives were plentiful, but not strong enough for the pups to forget the negatives. Most of the crew topped 40 miles per hour down from Shorebird pass. Then a nice woman allowed us to sleep in the church parking lot when we were tired and confused. Cub and Megan tried to keep up the good attitudes, even when things were hard for them. Cub had the most bike problems, but I think he was glad to get away from the barking during those quiet times to fix his own tires. Megan was the positive leader who tried to have the pack look at the good side of spending your summer with a group of people you don't truly know. In the church parking lot in Duck Lake, the group sat down and tried to resolve their issues. I could tell that Young Pup was getting the brunt of the complaints. Frenchy was the neutral pup. Slow Poke was quiet as well, however, he spoke up when the food selection issues came up. Socks and Smelly Hands were the most verbal, with Alpha Jr. combating many of their problems. The one solution that everyone agreed with was that the pack would set a goal each morning...agreed.

The goal for the following day, Sandy Land for the fireworks show.

Well, Sandy Land was the goal for other reasons as well. MAIL. This would be the first time for most of the cubs to get things from their families. Yeah Food was the first to realize that when we crossed the bridge we entered into a new state. The disgruntled pack cruised into towns and out, without the friendly demeanor that they previously radiated. Right when we passed through the last town before Sandy Land, a man told us some useful information. He suggested taking a different road into Sandy Land because of miles and miles of construction on our planned route. The once open eared pack was now too frustrated to go a few miles longer to get to the same place. Where was Jr.'s conversation on taking advice now?

The construction was miserable for Cub and I in the back. Megan is the better technical rider. Cub is faster, but not with obstructions in the way. Alpha Jr. and Slow Poke were just in front of us, when Cub rode right off the side of the thick sand and dirt road. Cub yelled when it happened, but he does have grace in wrecking. He landed on his side away from me, jumped up, and checked to make sure I was okay. We had flatted. The tube and tire was pinched to a stop by Cub's rack that had come loose. Jr. and Slow Poke came back to help get the bike back on the road. The bike probably weighed seven times more than me...it was not light with all of the food and supplies packed on.

Once fixed up, the four of us rode carefully through the construction and then flew on the last 5 miles of pavement before Sandy Land. We caught the rest of the group and headed straight to the Post Office. Just before closing we thought. Right when we got there, all of the pack realized in unison, the Post Office wouldn't be open, it was the Fourth of July. Yeah Food spoke out and said, "Look at us. We made through all of the terrible roads just to reach our goal. We made it. The mail will be here in the morning. And now we get to sleep in." Smiles appeared for the first time that day. Megan was relieved to see the attitudes change into positive happy people.

We ate pizza and ice cream near the lake, put our tents up in the local park, and then enjoyed the local Fourth of July fair.

Finally, the fireworks are done. Let's go to bed. Wait. Smelly Hands dropped a cookie. I see the group leaving, but I have to get the cookie. I run to grab the cookie. "Gu, GU," the pack calls out.

Chapter 7

July 6ᵗʰ

Cub growls at me, "Grrrrrr, GRRRRRR." I look at him. He growls again. I get into escape position: head low, butt high, ears down, eyes up. As he scoots toward me, he growls again. I take off. I'm running as fast as I can around him so he can't see me. He's fast...he jerks his body around pivoting on his knees to stop me halfway. "Grrrr." I take off the other way past the older humans. "Grrrrrrr." I get back into escape position.

Before we left Sandy Land, we picked up the mail. Megan went in and brought out an armful of envelopes and boxes. She passed them out to almost everyone...I even got one from Grandma. All I had to say was it tasted good. Unfortunately, we can't control who gets stuff and who doesn't. Slow Poke didn't get anything. He didn't seem down about it, but the rest of the pack received something. Cub shared Megan's, but at least that was something. Smelly Hands was the happiest with her care package which included candy, cookies and new magazines. Alpha Jr. received some jerky (yes!), and Frenchy's box had some special labels around it, and included all these candies I've never seen before. Young Pup got a letter that made him smile just a little differently, while Socks and Yeah Food seemed very content with their small packages. It doesn't take much when you miss your home. My home was here with Megan and Cub, so I didn't feel the homesickness that everyone else felt at one point or another.

Before we entered the next state we had some firsts. We ate at our first themed cafe...I wasn't a big fan of the theme - cats. Every wall had pictures of cats and every table had little cat statues. After lunch, another first. The pack used the Internet for the first time on the trip. The group stopped by the local library and spent a good hour catching up on their e-mails. I took a nap in the sunny grass yard outside of the library which was a treat. We then proceeded to go on our first so-called back road out of town. Then we hiked a bit off the road to get to this bridge. It was suspended in the air, above this river, and it moved as Megan carried me across. We were still in heavily forested areas and Cub said we should be for the next couple of days. The air had a cool moisture about it, and that made the smells come out of the woods. This little jaunt only took a few minutes, but it was a nice break from the norms of the trip so far.

On the bike, we actually went quite slow the next couple of days. Dawdling. We had a two big issues: no stores were open to get food supplies and rain the next morning. We didn't see many people out and about because of the weather. Cub made the goal for us to get to Billy...everyone laughed as I'm pretty sure that wasn't the name of that town either. After looking at the budget and where we were, Megan and Cub told the group we would stay in a motel that night. Everyone was thrilled. It didn't take much to make the pack happy...even if it was just for the short term. While in the motel, some of the pack went swimming, some just enjoyed the use of the pay phone, while others enjoyed time to talk to each other. Cub and Megan worked on the budget and tried to plan out the next couple of days. In the evening, the group gathered in one room and discussed the plan for the next day. The choice was to go North, South, or on a back road that looked the most direct...East. Not even a hesitation...East it was.

We started on the main road, but at the intersection, we went east. The road was empty of gas fumed vehicles, and there were many times when we were riding side by side. It felt like we were just hanging out on the road. The miles were passing by, and we hadn't seen a car, a house or any businesses. This also meant we had no place to get food or water. Oops. We got to a hard pack dirt road intersection. Where do we go? We debated for a while. As we were debating a truck drove by and we waved it down. He told us the only thing on the road was a ranch and they should have water. We thanked the young guy and we were off. The heat of the day was starting to take its toll. Everyone was beat. A wild fella jolted across the road in front of us with a rabbit in its mouth. He was probably related to me in some way, but I didn't care to find out. That rabbit probably weighed more than me. Finally, on the left side of the road we saw a modernized log cabin next to a well kept barn and another smaller cabin. We had reached the ranch. It stood out well because it was flat and without trees, but with trees surrounding the outskirts in the foothills.

Cub and I were last in the group, so we missed most of the introductions. To our luck though, they already had the jugs of water and vanilla cookies out waiting for us. There were three humans there. All of them about the same age as Grandma. The light colored hairy male was standing beside his mate in her overalls and ball cap. Staying with them was another male who I think was from the same state as Cub, Ohio. They proceeded to bring out sodas for all and more treats. Other than the humans, all of the other ladies and fellas were kind of nosy with me, but most of them were only a couple weeks old. They yipped and yapped, not much of a bark yet. There were seven of them, including the mother, and all were dark and light with a short nose. Then there was the nice older fella that was really dark with some slightly lighter areas around his mouth. He was the biggest of all of them. He probably weighed as much as Megan. He was very gentle with the young pups and had issues controlling his drool. The older humans offered us a dinner and a place to stay if we helped out around the ranch for the evening. Deal or no deal? Deal. Watching these city pups sweat for food was most excellent; splitting wood and piling it on the wood pile wasn't easy. They fed all of us well and set up a little campfire out back in the fire ring.

I'm getting hot. "Grrr." I take off again. Then Cub falls to the ground...I win. I pounce on him and softly bite his arm to show my dominance again.

Chapter 8

July 8th

    It just turned four o'clock in the afternoon and we all jump on our bikes. We take off. Cub's my pal for the day. We just topped off all of our water bottles, ate a quick snack, and made sure everything was packed on the bikes. Bikes are not allowed on this part of the road between eleven in the morning and four in the afternoon. The road is supposed to be narrow and filled with gas guzzlers. Going to the Sun road is the road that everyone talks about around these parts. It's going to top off at the highest point in all of our journey's at 6680 feet above sea level. The day is just perfect. Not too hot, not too cold, not too windy, too good to be told.

    Two days ago, after our short but sweet stay at the Ranch, some parted with tears from everyone's new temporary grandparents. I said bye to the mother and young-ones, then to old Darkie himself. After listening to everyone who lived there talk about the tough winters compared to the delightful summers, I appreciated the temperate weather where I'm from. Cub, Megan, and some of the young pups sat inside late at night listening to the elders talk about the below zero winter temperatures with relatively no personal contact. The pack has now changed their attitude again. They started the trip nervous and excited, which turned to tired but friendly, then bitter and homesick, and now was happy and motivated.

The next two days flew by. Nice people must grow on trees here in this part of the country, because the next day two people outside the grocery store offered us places to stay. We stayed at a place overlooking the Fishy Town we were in. Even though we looked to be running late the following day, we cranked through the miles and pulled into the National Park just in time to pick up the mail. We shopped a little at the stores near the entrance, buying gifts for friends and supplies for the next day's ride through the park. Our ride from here was easy once we decided on the campground. We pulled in and set up camp. The campground was in a heavily forested area and was quite busy. We were told this was the busiest time of year for the park, partly because it was closed during the winter months. Bear country signs were posted everywhere, so we stuffed all of our food in the closest bear box which was at another set of bikers' campsite. The bikers were a father and daughter duo that was heading cross-country as well. They were at a little faster pace than we were and were headed out to Going to the Sun road before 11 a.m., while we planned for the evening ascent.

Even though the attitudes were positive at this point, the cliques had formed. Smelly Hands, Socks, and Yeah Food were inseparable. Slow Poke, Alpha Jr. and Frenchy hung together most of the time. Young Pup was now the sniffer, but each of the groups showed frustration with him at one point or another. Sometimes I wondered if he's trying too hard to fit in because he's the youngest or if he usually gets what he wants and its just not happening within our pack. I didn't know. Cub and Megan have each talked to him casually, but I think he gets on their nerves sometimes too.

We rode a little bit in the morning, so that the evening ascent would be a little shorter. We rode to Fast Food Lodge and hung out for most of the day. The Lodge was old and big. Situated on the lake it had all of the amenities that anyone could want "camping". The lake was clear and cold; the view was clear and bold. Mountains, trees, abundant wildlife, and smells I couldn't believe, filled our senses. We ate lunch in the big yard in between the Lodge and the restaurant. A few of the pups decided it was their chance to eat a cooked meal and headed to the restaurant to get pizza. Others shot basketball next to the small one room post office. We all enjoyed a little ice cream at the general store across the road from the restaurant. It was a beautiful day. At one point all of us went to the side of the lake and enjoyed a friendly rock skipping contest. I know the part I liked best was the nap in the sun.

We already climbed the forested part of the road. It was shaded with more than just pine trees. Some of these trees have leaves. The road was normal width up to here, but we are starting to get to the narrower parts of the climb. Right now we are sitting on the rocks next to the road overlooking the first part of the road we climbed. Our plan is for Cub and me to stop every hour and wait for everyone to have a snack. The few leaved trees in front of us give us the shade to cool us off. It looks like from here on, there will be one side up against the wall of the mountain with the other being on the edge of a cliff, and only an old stone wall will keep us from plummeting down what we just climbed. Once we go around the hairpin turn in front of us, it looks like we will be on the edge of the old stone wall.

We are off again. Cub spins the cranks around at a pretty high cadence. I look back and we already have gaps on the pack behind us. Looking to the right, I'm high enough to easily see over the wheel-high wall to the depths below. We are going uphill at a steady steep grade with no room for the gas guzzlers to struggle past. I can hear and feel Cub's heart increasing in speed and strength. The pedals keep ticking around as the heart is in full force. The sweat is pouring out of his helmet onto his forehead as he wipes with his short fingered gloves so he can see in front of him. I'm bobbing up and down at a sweet little rhythm as he stands and pushes the bike to its limits. Ba dum, Ba dum, Ba dum almost two hundred times a minute. The rhythm sometimes lulls me to sleep; he stands then sits repeatedly. I look around and see waterfalls up in front, still a long way ahead. Snow patches fill the mountainous horizon. The sun has been lowering for a bit now, but we still have a couple of hours. Standing for one last push...Cub loves to climb. He pulls off to the side and leans his bike against the stone wall. We sit and wait. His heart is slowing as we sit and rest. I can barely feel it anymore. He stands up to cheer on Alpha Jr., he is the first pup to get to this point. I can't feel Cub's heartbeat anymore. Cub helps me to the ground to get a snack and water. He pulls out some gummy fish in a small individual pack. Gone in a second. Here come some of the others.

We're on our way again. The entire pack arrived with smiles at the last stop and ate their snacks. Now the heartbeats *are back. We cruise along as water drips off the walls to our left. People are out of their vehicles taking pictures. Others pass by with children sticking their hands out the windows to feel the weeping wall weep. The people in the sedan next to us cheers us on and offer Cub a Coke to drink. Cub declines but says thanks in between his deep breaths for air. Others we pass clap their hands and shout words of encouragement. Cub's heart is racing. He's given up on the sitting. He loves to stand on his bike, but he knows his heart works overdrive when he does. The sweat is still pouring off his long hair. I can feel the sweat off of his back. I can't believe he's sweating this hard as the sun continues to drop. Another waterfall is up ahead. Whoa. Water comes from up high on the left and cascades down under the road and down thousands of feet below. The wind picks up right as we pass the water. It is not a warm wind. Its air that feels like ice. Cub quickly shakes as the coldness creeps through his skin. I start shivering, but he warms as the cranks are still turning over.*

We are closing in on the top. The sun is quickly fading behind the mountains to our right. I look a little behind and to the right to see if anyone is close behind us. We are on the last right curve before it curves left and up to the visitor center at the top. Cub's heart is still thumping and sweat is still pouring out, but I'm shivering like crazy. We look ahead and see a dozen cars parked to the side. Most of the humans were out looking with binoculars and cameras at the hill to the left. Cub and I look over. Beautiful white mountain goats are standing in the snow patches to the left. Cub keeps cranking with a big smile on his face. I keep looking back at those goats. The cold air is now blowing in our face and Cub pushes the pedals a little more unevenly; pushing with all of his power to finish up the climb.

Cub's heartbeat has faded and both of us are covered up in our warmest attire. A pair of windbreaker pants for Cub and a warm fleece hat to sit in for me. We are standing here taking a picture of each person finishing the long beautiful climb. The family of humans next to us asks us where we are from and why we are riding. A few of the pups answer the questions. Here comes Megan riding just behind Slow Poke. They have huge smiles on their faces as Slow Poke punches his fist in the air. That's right.

Chapter 9

July 9th

"Just keep the ball away from me! Keep the ball away from me!" I tell the pups. The sound of the ball dribbling on the hard pavement sends shivers down my spine. I'm still a little scared of that ball. First of all, its bigger than me; secondly, I can't seem to guess where it's going to bounce or be thrown to next. I'm standing on Megan's feet, pushing my body up against her legs, looking up at her in between the hideous thumps hoping she will pick me up. Two feet on each of hers, hoping she will keep the ball away from me.

After Going to the Sun, our highest point in elevation, we had a long downhill to the much talked about campground. Now, in my opinion, the downhill was good, but many of the pups were slightly disappointed that it wasn't as steep or long as the side that we went up. Basically, we didn't get as close to 45 miles per hour and we thought we would. This didn't faze them, as they were tired and ready to crash for the evening. Luckily, we all snagged some pizza from the one spot that was open that late at night. The Baby Shampoo Campground was one of the nicest spots we've paid for so far. I don't think it really would have mattered, because once the pups laid their head down, they were out. No rolling around. No talking. No giggling. No walking in circles until the spot was just right. They were out.

Breakfast the next morning looked amazing. The food at the restaurant was apparently family style. I guess the deal with family style was that you order things the whole group wants, and then everyone shares off the main platters. The group didn't know. Each ordered their personal favorite. Then, when the platters big enough to hold an 18 pound turkey were placed on the table, everyone just stopped and stared. I was watching with Cub through the window. Yeah Food brought us piles of food right away. Slow Poke seemed to be in heaven. The long table seating 8 of them was filled in at every spot with some sort of food. It was just like meals at Grandma's. Cub and I enjoyed our food and the crisp cool breeze on the porch. Unfortunately, the meal didn't seem to re-energize the group. Instead it put everyone into a food coma. They all looked like zombies, but at least they were happy zombies.

The ride that day was probably harder than it seemed, but

48

after the ride the day before, the fantastic breakfast, and stocking up at the local store, it was a breeze. Speaking of breezes, the breeze had changed. It wasn't cool anymore. It was warmer and drier. We cruised as a cohesive pack up the first five mile hill and then enjoyed the downhill to our destination. As we pulled into town, I noticed it wasn't packed with humans and their oil tankers. Many buildings had boarded up windows, while others looked like they could barely stand. The trees had disappeared and dust passed in front of us as we rode.

Our first stop was the local grocery store. We didn't know where to park our 9 bikes. One of the grocery store workers gave us a hard time, saying we were interfering with their "real" customers. Finally, we were allowed to park near the huge metal garbage cans. Then an older male stumbled toward us. He had a long coat with straggly hair. He started to yell at some of the male pups and then stumbled over to the females. Cub and Megan quickly moved towards the females. At that moment, I was worried the morale of the group might quickly shift to the negative. Then a young adult male jumped in front of the stumbler and said "Go home." The stumbler slowly drifted away. The young man apologized and said that was his uncle who struggles with keeping himself "away from the bottle". The young man looked similar to the stumbler, but had a strong smile.

His skin was darker, and his really dark long hair and eyebrows highlighted his face. He continued to talk with Cub and me until Megan finished purchasing the supplies for the following day's epic ride. The young man told us this weekend was the Indian Days Fair and said we could camp near his family for the night. That was more like it. A perfect place to lay our heads.

The dribbling stopped. All of the smaller local pups, the Weiners, who were playing with our whole pack were now our escorts through the tents. We are in the field next to the museum on the west end of town. I'm hanging with the whole pack. I keep smelling all of these great smells. Food is everywhere. The Weiners introduce our group to everyone. It was great. A little food here...a little food there...many things I've never tried before. Cub turns his nose to many things because he's picky, but he still ate enough for two. Smelly Hands and Socks just headed off to check out some of the crafts different groups were selling. Yeah Food, Frenchy, and Alpha Jr. just saw that Slow Poke, Cub, Megan and Young Pup were headed toward the drumming sounds and follow behind. I don't like loud sounds. Luckily, Megan stops far enough away to hear, but thankfully not too close. I'm staying with her. The chants and beats are filling the food laced air and we just sit here and enjoy it. The sun is starting to set. Past all of the drummers and chanters, I can see the bikes with their flags on the horizon. Teepee's were to the right of them and in the distance the mountains we had conquered were just silhouettes. Clouds were moving by, changing shades with the lowering sun. Night was coming upon us. It'll be bedtime soon.

Chapter 10

July 10th

    "Let's not go in there" I quietly state to the group.

    "Come on. Let's go," Alpha Jr. says. The group quickly lay their bikes under the little overhang on the old abandoned grain building. The clouds around us are closing in. Lightning falls from the sky and strikes the ground in all directions. The cloudy day is now producing the threatening storms that the locals expected the next couple of afternoons. We all climb up onto the porch, and every one of the pups squeeze into the building. Megan and I make sure everyone is inside. The long abandoned building is almost talking to us.

    I'm pretty sure it just said, "Get out before I fall." I hate thunder and lightning. I keep trying to hide in between Megan and Cub. Most of the pups are sitting and listening to the building crack and creek, but Young Pup and Slow Poke are wandering around. Cub seems a little freaked out by the storm above us, so I cuddle up to him a little more. Megan is talking to

Socks and Smelly Hands, not even noticing the building could collapse at any moment.

Young Pup happily yells out, "I found a few dead rats." Everyone jumps up. Boy, I hope this storm is almost over.

The road from the colorful Native American town has been the long, longer and longest stretch of straight road I've ever been on. I couldn't tell you much about the route other than that. We did go through a pretty big town and then a smaller one, but spent little time in either. We went to the grocery store, ran in and got supplies. Threw some food into our mouths and back onto the bikes. This whole process has improved with efficiency compared to the early days that already seemed months ago.

We knew there wouldn't be any mountains in our near future. Everywhere we looked on the ride, to the North, East or South, we saw fields and fields of dry grasslands. Cub led the pack, while Megan and I hung out in the back. With the road being pretty straight with just slight inclines and declines, we could see everyone in front of us all day long. The day had been different in other ways too. The weather drastically changed when the wind picked up. Then all of a sudden the wind died and we could smell the rain in the air. We all could tell we had a limited time to ride before something was going to happen.

Pack emotions started to drift back to the other side of the attitude scale. We expected some issues, since it was our first attempt at 100 miles, which would be our first century. We were still behind on our summer schedule. This was our chance to get miles in while the wind and the land weren't against us. Socks, Alpha Jr., and Frenchy wanted to ride as fast as possible so that we would have more time off of the bike. Yeah Food wasn't feeling the best with a slight cold and was having neck and shoulder pain as the day went on. Young Pup was leeching onto Slow Poke and Smelly Hands. Slow Poke and Smelly Hands tried to ride at a pace they were comfortable with, but the stronger rider, Young Pup, just drafted behind them. Smelly Hands was obviously irritated by the drafting leech. Drafting only works if everyone takes their turn. Smelly hands felt Young Pup should have taken his turn in front.

We just pulled Smelly Hands away from Young Pup...the rat spotting pushed Smelly Hands over the edge. Luckily, the thunder, lightning and rain is starting to subside. The pack is now heading out to the porch facing the Southern skies. Most of us just sit on the edge facing the lightning in the distance slowly move away from us. We've lost a couple of hours, but the view right now is most excellent. All the emotions from a moment ago

have subsided with the rain. We jump on our bikes.

The pavement is dark with puddles in the most unavoidable places for some and in the best placed places for others. I like the puddles. The sun is right at that stage where everything changes shades. The glare and gleaming rays bounce off each puddle in its own unique way. The blaring winds are gone and replaced with a soft warm side breeze. It's great. I can see everyone in the pack just looking around in amazement. Water is splashing up on the back of my head from our bike, but then getting splashed in my eyes from Slow Poke just in front of us. Megan slows a tad, just enough for Slow Poke and Smelly Hands to have their own splashing room. I have to squint my eyes to see. I feel like the guy on "The Matrix" moving my body in unbelievable ways to avoid the water bullets heading right toward my face and body. Unfortunately, I've been hit many times and feel like a soaked rat.

I see a town closing in on us. The darkness isn't totally here yet, but will be shortly. Cub just came out of a store and said to follow him. The pack slowly moves. A few blocks away, we see a park. Yes. Cub stops at the first picnic table and pulls out of the bags he was carrying, five gallons of ice cream and spoons for all, except me. I'm waiting patiently. Maybe if I do my imitations and look cute someone will share with me. I put my butt on the ground, sit up as straight as possible, and put my paws close to my body. Cub reaches out his spoon with some vanilla ice cream. Yeah! He always falls for my meerkat impressions.

I'm in the sleeping bag on the picnic table trying to go to asleep. A few minutes ago, a nice tall person from across the street informed us of the morning sprinklers. He told Megan where they went off and how to avoid them. I couldn't imagine getting woken up by cold, wet sprinklers. Cub is making sure everyone is out of sprinklers way. The darkness is upon us and Cub climbs onto the table and hides in our bag. We should be safe up here.

Alpha Jr. yells out, "102...let's go for 103 tomorrow."

Frenchy and Yeah Food almost in unison yell back, "NO WAY."

The pack yells and yips a few more times at the moon, but then the pack falls silent. Their calls are replaced by the sounds of the night.

56

Chapter 11

July 14th

I can't wait to get out of this State. Cub just said it is only a couple more miles before we cross the state line. We are pushing to get to a place to stay for the night. I don't know if we'll make it to the big town or not. The wind makes our bikes feel like they are glued in place. Some of the pups are trying to push a hard gear, but their legs don't want to complete their cycle. The other pups are spinning their pedals really fast, but they aren't going anywhere. This is our fifth day in a row with terribly hard headwinds. I'm hiding my head behind Cub's, hoping he will break the wind. The pups are in a tight pack, but the toll of the wind is bearing down on them. By looking at the sun, I can see we have about two hours left before darkness. We just want to make it somewhere besides these grasslands to rest. When I stick my head out to see what's coming, it's all a little blurry. Cub and I slow down at least a mile or two an hour so I tuck my head back behind his.

We were told by everyone that going West to East across the country was the best way, because we would have the winds at our back most of the way. So far we have had one good tailwind day. The headwinds since our 102 miles have been torture. I could imagine those crouching wolves in the cold of winter with their ears laid back and the blowing snow pushing against them. That's what it felt like except with hot air. Our mouths had been dry, our water bottles empty, and our enjoyment blown away. The grasslands on every side provide us with very little protection from the beating we're taking. We were warned about mosquitoes, but that wasn't an issue, as the winds kept them at bay.

However, for every beating we've taken on our bikes, we've been lucky enough to have super nice people willing to help at every stop. The day after the century, Smelly Hands had a problem with her wheel. We knew about broken spokes, and this wasn't the first time we had to try to fix them. This time it was different - it wasn't one spoke, it was five. Something had fallen off her bags and got stuck in her wheel. We didn't have tools or parts to replace that many spokes, so we headed to a bike shop the first night. The mechanic took off Cub's temporary contraption and told us he could take care of the problem in the morning. We had to stop by before heading out of town. We slept at the park in the middle of the town. Rain came down off and on all night. Most of the pups slept in tents on the gazebo, but Cub and I hid in some playground pipes to stay dry.

The next morning we were set to take off, but the mechanic had some family issues and had a young pup working the shop. The young pup didn't seem to know what to do, but Cub and Megan said to trust him...so we did. We shopped while waiting, but the wheel still wasn't done. Megan decided to send the group ahead. She, Socks and Smelly Hands would wait, then catch up by lunch. I went with Cub. Cub and the rest of the pups took off to battle the wind and finally stopped at a traveling home campground to eat lunch. We waited. Then we waited some more. Hours passed and finally the three females pulled in when they saw our bikes. The young pup at the shop didn't know what he was doing, so he finally called the owner who came and fixed the bike for free. While at the campground, a traveling couple in their movable home listened to our battles and then wanted to help out. They bought us all some ice cream and treats. It was great. We were running late, so we had to eat the ice cream on the bike. With the wind blowing, the ice cream melted fast. The pack looked like a mess. I would catch a drip or two as they flew by my face, but Cub was a sharer and would reach over his shoulder with the cone and let me lick off all of the melt I could. I'm pretty sure, we lost more than we ate.

Over the next two nights we were invited into people's houses to stay the night. The first night, our pack tried to settle down in a spot near the Got Milk River, but forecasts of grapefruit sized hail brought many people to our aide. The next night, another horrible sounding forecast sent hoards of people our way to invite us inside for the night. Both nights we were treated with the best hospitality you could ask for. We slept on the floor, but were able to cook pancakes on a stove and have hot chocolate refills. That was most excellent. Now the pack had multiple personalities: gracious off the bike versus frustrated on the bike. Luckily, at night, the gracious faces appeared. I couldn't tell you what everyone else did while inside, because after the food was put away I went straight to bed. Boy do I love rugs.

We've made it. This is the biggest town we've seen for a long time. We see a college in part of the town, and many old brick buildings along the main strip. We had been separated for a bit as some of the pack turned off into town a different way, but we finally regrouped. I think Megan and Alpha Jr. are talking to a gentleman with glasses on. Things are blurry, but it looks like

he has glasses on. Alpha Jr. hurries over to us and the pack and says the gentleman has room for all of us to stay. Another battle and another savior.

Chapter 12

July 17ᵗʰ

Looking at the bike, I don't know if there is much hope. I'm not a mechanic, but I do know when something is bent in that direction it usually doesn't work. Most of the pack is lying in the grass, eating the snacks they bought inside the gas station. Cub, Megan, Slow Poke and I look at the bike and decide we have to take off the rear dérailleur. Cub pulls out one of his many folding tools and quickly unbolts the dérailleur from its hanger. He folds back the number 5 allen key and unfolds the chain breaker. Without a dérailleur, Slow Poke is going to have to ride a single gear or singlespeed until this can be permanently fixed. Cub shortens the chain, so that it doesn't flop off of the chainrings. We're working hard. This is the third major bike problem we've had the past three days. Grease is on everyone's arms, fingers and faces. Finally, Slow Poke jumps on the bike in the parking lot and rides around. It will work, for now.

After we left the college town, we had a major decision to make. Do we stay on the same major road then drop down to Movie Town and our next mail drop, or do we go south to the freeway and hope for a bike shop in the bigger towns along the way. A day before, the dilemma would not have mattered, but as soon as we left the college town we had more broken spokes and a very annoying rear rack bolt that somehow bent and left the rack holding up the baggage now leaning against the wheel. Cub jimmied it so the rack wouldn't rub against the wheel, but it still needed to be fixed. We only had one chance to make our decision. So the group decided to head toward the freeway where the bigger towns lined the map.

The weather got hotter and the afternoon storms packed a solid punch. We were lucky the first day after college town. The rain storms held off 'till the evening. Riding in the heat through hills of wild grasses seemed familiar, but this time the wind did not fight us for every pedal stroke and the hills changed ever so slightly as we rode. We passed small towns and ate some greasy food at an old drive-in diner. We crossed a neat metal bridge just before we turned right, off of the main road, to find our resting hole. We were a bit worried because the sign said one mile; however, the road was just dirt and we couldn't see anything that looked like a campground. Then we topped the hill. The flat deserted campground was fine and dandy. Plenty of room for us to spread out our tents, and the pups said the bathroom was a fancy port-a-pottie. That night we had plenty of time to cook our food over the alcohol stoves we carried. The sunset was amazing, and it was followed by the most impressive lightning storm yet. Lightning seemed to surround us for over an hour, but nothing seemed to be heading right toward us. Then it hit. I was in the tent with Cub hoping I could fall asleep before the lightning struck our tent.

The next day everyone seemed to be back to the positive side of the attitude scale. Unfortunately, that didn't last long. We left our country's natural beautiful grasslands for flatter grasslands with gas guzzlers that whizzed by us. We met a truck with cyclists who were working on a mountain bike trail around the outskirts of the Presidential park. They stopped to fill up our waters, which was much appreciated, but other than that the motorized vehicles skimmed by us one too many times. That was all before the freeway. Cub and Megan were hoping Famous Authorville would have a bike shop to help us out. It didn't exist. At that moment, the pack was at an all-time low. Alpha Jr. was arguing with the females, Young Pup was adding just enough words to make everyone mad, and Frenchy stomped away from the group. Yeah Food's neck and back were still making her miserable and Slow Poke just quietly sat there looking dejected. Then the wind picked up and that put the icing on the cake. It was a long day. Getting to sleep sounded like the best thing for the day, but the wind blew one tent into the creek and my tent, with just me inside, was blown around like a tumbleweed.

The next day wasn't great, but at least there was a slight tailwind to make the riding easier. The freeway wasn't too bad, but our luck with bike shops was awful. While I tried to enjoy the riding, I think Megan tried to keep everyone away from each other to let their frustrations settle. The one destination that was peaking everyone's interest was marked by signs that advertised the "World's Biggest Cow". It was getting late, but the group unanimously decided to head off the freeway for a couple of miles to see the World's Biggest Cow. I don't even know how to start explaining it, but it was a very big cow that overshadowed the small new town. I couldn't see it quite clearly. It didn't have any smells like all of the normal sized cows we had passed.

His legs are spinning as fast as they can to stay up with the group. Slow Poke and his singlespeed are at a disadvantage with this nice gradual downhill. We are heading to the biggest city on the freeway stretch. I'm looking forward and can see

Slow Poke's legs turning over, but I can't really see anyone else very well. The city in front of us must be foggy or something. Things are all so blurry. The wind is blowing my ears forward into my eyes while we cruise behind the group. Apparently, everyone else has gone full blast to get to the Hawaiian Wood campground. We pass the city and Megan looks happier now that the group is together again. We turn left and everyone seems satisfied that the campground is in sight. At the campground, Megan stops by a pay phone that has a phone book and turns the pages quickly as darkness is now setting. She jots down something and we head into the building. An older gentleman is sitting in front of a television. He looks up and slowly walks over towards us.

"Nice companion you have there," he says to Megan.

Megan says, "Yep, he is."

The tents are all set in one campground spot closest to the basketball court. My eyes are tired of this foggy and blurry day. I'm ready for sleep. Alpha Jr., Slow Poke, Frenchy and Cub are shooting while everyone else is reading or writing. I'll just sneak in to Cub's tent and get my rest on. I move the sleeping bag around a bit to make it a little more comfortable and I burrow into the hole. Boy its nice and cozy in here.

Chapter 13

July 18th

Cub just went inside again with Slow Poke. Where is he going? "Wait for me. Wait for me," I call out as loud as I can. Young Pup is holding Cub's pack.

He says, "Calm down Gu. Calm down." I'm moving my feet around so I can see better. I can't see him. Where did Cub go? I'm flailing my body around to try to get over to the door Cub went in. Young Pup is trying to restrain me, but I want to know where Cub is. It's still foggy around and I can't really see where he went anymore. I keep calling out for Cub, but I'm not getting any response. Finally, Young Pup quits trying to restrain me. I'm off. Running around looking for Cub. Where's he at? Where's he at? I look up and down. I sniff the air hoping his smell filters through. Someone opens the door and I sprint in. A hand comes down to greet me, but I don't have time for that. Where's Cub?

Today was supposed to be a nice, easy day. We left the
campground after the pack shot a game of hoops. We headed
south toward the city and turned right into an industrial strip. We
cruised though a pretty big strip where the bike shop used to be.
The key words there were "used to be." A young guy at the
sandwich shop across the way said the bike shop just recently
closed. He was nice enough to give us directions to the mall
which had a sporting goods store. We took off, after thanking
the young man. The pack was frustrated and happy at the same

time. Alpha Jr., Yeah Food, Smelly Hands and Young Pup were stoked with the idea of being able to shop. Time passed us by, the easy day was becoming a rushed afternoon. We filtered into the mall on the southern end of the city. The mall had a huge sporting goods store. Cub and the broken bike gang followed him in. They soon came out and gave us the news. The mechanics at the store said it would be a couple of hours. Half of the pack yelled out in excitement while the others didn't seem to care. Megan ordered pizzas for the pack and we all decided to meet back here at the bikes at one o'clock to eat. We would make more plans at that time.

I just sat with Cub out in the warm sun peering through the fog. I was confused on how warm it was, because it seemed so foggy. We just laid in the grassy strip next to the endless parking lot. After our short dog nap, the group all slowly showed their faces. Pizza was always a treat. I love it, anytime. Most of the pack scarfed the pizza down as if it wasn't dead yet and would take off if they didn't eat fast enough. Cub checked on the bikes. I always got last choice on foods and sometimes no choice. Meerkat pose was always a crowd pleaser; pepperonies came at me left and right. Cub came back out and informed all of us that it would be a little longer. Time seemed to slow down. The shoppers were off for the hunt and the others were trying to avoid the afternoon heat by resting in the few shaded areas. Time was not by our side any more. Days behind already, we needed to ride. We had to get somewhere. At that point in the day, we'd only gone South and West. I might be wrong, but if my calculations were still correct, the Atlantic Ocean was East. Just a few minutes before Slow Poke's bike was to be done, a decision was made. Everyone got on their bikes. Megan decided to start the progression and head back to the freeway to see if we could get forty or so miles in before dark. They all took off except for Young Pup, Slow Poke, Cub and I. We had to pay for the services.

This place is packed. Clothes, boxes and people fill almost every spot. I don't get many chances to head into stores like this. There are straight paths in most directions, then curved paths that have no real destination. I'm running around checking every corner, smelling under every box, listening for the crackle in Cub's voice or his bike shoes clicking on the hard ground. Maybe there will even be indentions in the wood floor from his cleats. Why is it cloudy in here? I don't get it. Where is he at? People keep reaching their hands out to greet me, but I just run in opposite directions. AAAAAAAAH. There must be another part of this store. I can't see any bikes or smell any bike

grease. I wonder where they are. I put my nose to the air. Hmm...I can smell food. Maybe they are getting more food. If anyone is, it would be Cub and Slow Poke. I'm running through all of the humans speeding around, not paying much attention to each other, except for the juveniles who can't keep their eyes off each other. There's the food. There's the food.

I couldn't find any evidence of Cub or Slow Poke near the food, but all of this searching is making me hungry, so I scarf down some food lying around. People everywhere were offering me food, but they just kept it in their hands. I just let them keep it. Where could they be? I run around. Is that them? I run toward them...the two guys turn around. Nope. I take off the other way. The wiener pups keep pointing at me, giggling, and trying to offer me food, but I need to find Cub. Oh no! Some humans all dressed the same are starting to come towards me. Run. I am going as fast as I can, avoiding all of the feet that are coming from every direction. Some are fast, some slow, some can't walk a straight line and others are stop and go. Here come the matching humans. They are trying to surround me. My ears are laid back, my butt is low and I'm ready to escape. The key is to always change speed and directions and to bite if necessary. At least other fellas tell me the biting works. I've never tried it myself.

I feel like I've been searching for days. I've been lucky to avoid the suits so far. Here they come again. Oh no, they have some sheets with them. They're trying to trap me. What am I going to do? There is a small cave under the stairs they can't fit into. Running as fast as I can, I scoot by one of the suits. There is just enough clearing for me to make it. Safety for now. All I see are these unfamiliar faces reaching out to me, but I'm just out of reach. I'm still smelling everyone, hoping Cub's smell will reach my nose. Some loud speaker thingy keeps calling for something, but with all of the static and feedback, I can't understand what it is saying. Maybe Cub is trying to call me. Every muscle in my body is shaking because I'm so nervous. I don't want the suits to get me and I want Cub to come back. Wait...what's that smell? What's that smell? I don't see him, but I can smell him. Where's he at? Where's he at? The suits' faces all disappear and there's Cub. I scoot out and kiss him all over his face. He's shaking nervously as well. I'm so happy to see him. Looking around, I notice there are hundreds of humans all facing us. I can't see their faces very well, but I can feel their eyes staring. It doesn't matter...I'm safe with Cub.

Chapter 14

July 19th

I wonder if he can get back on to Slow Poke's wheel. Come on, Cub. Cub flicks his right hand to shift gears without letting go of the brake hoods. He seems to be struggling, flailing his body back and forth to push the slightly harder gear. There we are, right about 6 inches behind Slow Poke's back wheel. It feels like we are being sucked towards Slow Poke, then Cub relaxes a little bit. Each pedal stroke is hurting Cub. His body is tighter and he sounds like he is whimpering when he isn't shouting out directions or support. We have the best spot in the group now. Slow Poke is flying. Cub has had a hard time staying behind Slow Poke's wheel for the draft. Slow Poke looks relaxed and confident. He's pushing a gear in the big chainring and his pedaling looks smooth, almost without effort. Slow Poke has been up here for a long time. He flicks his left elbow out to the left without missing a stroke. Cub sees it and starts to pass him on the left side with Young Pup following behind our wheel. Slow Poke relaxes with a few soft pedal strokes and he drifts backwards on our right. He catches on to Young Pup's wheels and here we go up front. Cub is hurting, but still pushing the gear to keep the fast pace the two young pups have maintained their turns at the front. The whimpering continues, but the pace does not ease.

I stick my head up to Cub's left shoulder to get a better view. I can't see much, but the wind on my face feels great. I lean forward and squint my eyes to see if that helps my vision, but to no avail. Cub continues to whimper until he flicks his left elbow and relaxes for a few seconds with the soft pedal strokes as Young Pup and Slow Poke cruise by. We drift back to the left and catch the back wheel. Cub yells out, "There's a B.K. at the next exit. It's been an hour." Young Pup continues at the pace as he and Slow Poke nod their heads in acknowledgment. We slow a tad as we exit the freeway; the Burger King is right there. We pull into the parking lot and slow to a stop. This is our feed zone.

We ended up staying at the Hawaiian Wood campground again, because of the endless search for Cub yesterday. It was too late for us to catch up to the rest of the pack. Young Pup kept

74

telling Cub he was sorry, while Cub kept saying "no worries". The four of us ate a big dinner last night and then shot basketball for a bit, all in between the phone calls Cub made to his boss. He was trying to get messages to Megan. Without cell phones this was the process that took time. The pack had made it just over 40 miles. Their progress was slow. When they first regrouped they saw no sign of us. Luckily, Cub knew we weren't going to catch them for the night and asked a trucker to pass the message to call the boss and passed on what had happened. The message was passed and the emergency process of calling the boss was in progress.

When we woke in the morning, Cub went straight to the phone, however, the process was long from being over. Cub pondered many options for the day. Do we hitch a ride for the four of us? Do we pay for a rent-a-car? Do we have the group wait for us? Do we just ride to a final destination? Questions were being kicked around like a hacky sack. Finally, after a couple of hours of calling and waiting, Cub told his boss, "We're riding...we'll catch up to them by nightfall." Cub went over to the pups and told them the plan. He said we are going to catch the group before bed. He then told them to go buy two subs for each of them and to eat one now and save the other one. Then he said, "we'll stop every hour to eat and to use the restroom. Drink a bottle of water an hour. We have to haul." He then proceeded to tell them the rest of the pack was going to do 100 miles. The looks were almost of disbelief, until they realized he was serious and he believed they could do it.

Young Pup said, "Hey, we'll have a strong tailwind." And the journey was on its way.

We were told of a road that paralleled the freeway for the first 20 something miles, so we took it. I'd never seen Young Pup and Slow Poke work so well together with Cub. The three of them looked like a team in a time trial. Each would take their turn in front, while the others stayed in the slipstream of the leader. We went over 20 miles for the first hour. It was unreal. Just as Cub said, we were going to stop every hour to eat and pee. And we did. Cub wanted everyone to eat about 200 calories per hour, so that no one would bonk, or lose all energy and movement. The food was easily thrown in, and we were off again. The next hour coincided with a small town off the freeway that had a gas station with a convenience store. Cub bought everyone a sports drink and I took my chance to pee and go number two. We got back on the bikes and we were off.

Young Pup was full of energy and positive words. He took the longest pulls at the front of the group and then cheered on Slow Poke and Cub when they needed some words of encouragement. It seemed everyone needed those today. Early in the day, everyone flew with the wind, feeling as if it was pushing us toward our goal. Now as the day went on, Young Pup's energy in words were there, but his legs had a harder time keeping up. Slow Poke had been the surprise, quietly pushing the big gear with the most consistency and efficiency. His name wouldn't fit him long if he continued at today's pace. Cub, however, was the one who was struggled the most. His feet were killing him. Cub liked to ride without socks, but the past two weeks of rain had affected his shoes and feet. They shrunk on top of where the toes go, and now his toes were being rubbed raw. With his shrunk shoes and the length of our ride, the biggest problem of all was that along the freeway, a few feet into the shoulder of the lanes, where these unavoidable grooves cut out of the pavement called rumble strips. They might be great for keeping the person behind the wheel awake, but they weren't for the cyclist with the shrunken shoes. His whimpering was like clockwork, occurring between 9 and 1 o'clock on each stroke. Unfortunately, there were two clocks that he was winding.

We are back to the front. Today's pack has been amazingly strong, even when their bodies aren't. The wind is blowing steady at our backs and we can see for miles in front of us. We thought we had flat straight roads in the last state, but they were curvy mountainous roads compared to the ones we've been on this week. Young Pup takes his pull. The pulls are longer, but are slower than earlier in the day. I can't believe that after 7 stops, we are still cruising at this pace. The sun is starting to set and the only fliers to pass us were the truckers. It can't be much further. Cub is whimpering and starts to fall back off the young pups. He pulls his feet out of his shoes, and places his feet on top of them as they are still connected to the pedals. He sighs with relief. Young Pup notices the upcoming town and points it out to us. We're almost there. I'm so tired. I never thought that I could fall asleep on a bike, but there have been times today that I have. My head just slowly drifts down onto Cub's shoulder, as my eyes start to close shut. Cub stands up to pedal a little faster past the exit ramp and I wake up again. AAAHHH! Cub's foot slips off the shoe. We're going to fall. He holds tight to the handlebars with both hands, but one foot is dragging on the road as we weave in and out of the freeway lanes. Cub's straddling the top tube or crossbar and his face has fear covering it. What do I do? What do I do? I'm preparing for impact. The bike starts to slow and straighten up. Cub gets his foot on the shoe and completely stops the bike. We didn't wreck. Whew. Young Pup and Slow Poke are amazed that we didn't visit the pavement. We start off again.

There's the bikes. There's the group. The pack begins to howl in appreciation and Megan comes over and gets me off the bike. I'm shaking with excitement. Cub hollers out, "143 miles."

Megan says jokingly, "That's it?"

Chapter 15

July 21ˢᵗ

Megan, stay here. I'm standing right on Megan's feet, pushing my body up against her legs. The tall hairy guy keeps talking, but I can't listen to him. I'm nervously shaking and can't control my muscles enough to calm them down. The room is way too clean and there is no place for me to go and hide. The man offers me some treats. He's only doing that because he wants something from me. "Megan, pick me up. Pick me up," I quietly say, but I think she's trying to size up the big guy in front of her. Finally, Megan picks me up and she's trying to calm me down. I just want to get out of here as quick as possible before they pick and prod at me.

I don't remember laying my head down two nights ago, but I know I slept great. Cub and I slept in. The following morning when we woke, everyone was awake and all packed up. We hurried to catch up with everyone while they casually ate breakfast. Most of them just had some sort of cereal while others ate some of the fruit. Cub threw in some of his doughnuts he never shares and then fed me some of my normal breakfast (which is usually my biggest meal of the day). The food quickly disappeared.

The ride that day was short and sweet with a slight tailwind. We headed to a pretty well known area for the movie-goers in the group and with Cub's silly town names, I don't know which movie he's referring to when he calls it Freaky Cold Movie Town. He also said there is another city just across state-line he called Moopshead, which had some reference to the Bubble Boy episode of Seinfeld. The pack was in a hurry to get to the city for many reasons, but the most important was that the following day was our day off. The pack dynamics had changed in the past couple of days. Attitudes were pushed to the side and even Young Pup seemed to be working for the benefit of the group. Slow Poke pushed the pace in the front, never drifting back behind more than the front three riders. Frenchy was excited for the upcoming mail drop. He expected some food back from home and was told by his dad that it would be here without doubt. Every time I looked around the group, Socks and Alpha Jr. were always near each other. Yeah Food and Smelly Hands were getting along almost like sisters.

The campground wasn't too far away from the bike shop. Baseball games were going on near the entrance and the place was filled with people participating in different outdoor activities. It was great. We hadn't been to many places where a lot of people were out and about doing things, possibly because we usually arrived at most towns and cities at sunset rather than late afternoon. There was a river cruising right by the campground and plenty of grassy places under the trees where we placed our dens. Cub was the happiest to get off the bike and take off his shoes. Everyone just stood around and stared at his feet. All of his toes were swollen and red, mostly from open wounds. The brown shoes now had dark red seeping through the top. He grabbed his sandals and was on his way to the phone, limping pretty bad. Over on the pay phone, Megan was already busy taking care of business. The dens were put up and everyone relaxed and ate a nice tomato basil pasta.

After waking up in the morning, the pack went to the movies and shopped at thrift stores. They looked forward to the Mexican dinner at one of the local restaurants. Everyone showered. Earlier in the trip there were times where some of the pups wouldn't shower for the whole week, but that phase had ended and whenever they got a chance to shower, they did. I couldn't recognize most of the people dressed in non-riding clothes, but everyone was still looking a little fuzzy. Megan and Cub kept talking to each other in private, and would quit talking when I came over. I wondered what was up.

I don't need to see the vet. I'm fine. Megan sits me up and the lady vet lets me check out the tool in her hand. She's trying to talk nicely to me, but I'm not paying attention to her words because I want to know what she's going to do. Megan hands me over to the tall hairy guy and I freeze. I'm gonna stare at her and make sure she doesn't do anything that will hurt. I stare at her intently. She turns off the lights in the room and then flashes this bright light in my eyes. "I can't see! Turn it off its too bright!" She turns the room lights on again and is playing flinch. She quickly moves her hands toward my eyes and I sit there frozen. I don't flinch. The man holds my head still and I'm ready to bite if necessary. She drops in some liquid into my eyes. What is she doing? She's touching my eyes with something, but I can't feel it. Are we done yet?

We've left the scary place and we rode to the pet store. Yeah. I get something new. Wait. I don't want any clothes....no...no...not the Doggles. Ahhh. I don't want to wear sunglasses. At least pick out the right size. Those are too big. Finally, these fit. I reach up to try to take them off. Megan says,

"No Gu." I guess I have to wear them.

Megan and I get on the bike and we're off. These aren't too bad. We are flying because we have to get back to get ready for dinner. We pass people left and right. On the bike path, everyone is pointing at us. Haven't they seen someone with sunglasses before? We just passed a small pup riding his bike and I heard him say, "Now that's funny." I hate these glasses.

Chapter 16

July 25th

    "Why don't you take this road, instead of that one," the older lady says to Cub, "This one is the road I ride my Harley on. It's more scenic and better than going that way." Cub nods his head in agreement. Hair up in a bun, the lady reaches her hand out toward me. I sniff her. She's been making cookies. Where're the cookies? Where're the cookies? Licking her hand, she realizes I'm a bit hungry. She waddles on over to the counter in between the living room and kitchen and picks up something covered with aluminum foil. Cookies? Cookies? Cub places me on the floor and I'm off. I want some. Down here. I want some. Boy, I'm hungry.

    Cub is shaking his head and says, "It must be the meds. All he wants to do is eat."

This week has flown by. Since departing on our day off, we've been rained on daily. We pulled away from Hall-of-Famer campground and the rain started to drop. I couldn't tell where we were going. My Doggles didn't shed the water very well and all day I just watched drops splat against my lens and then slide down. I could tell how hard it was raining by how quickly the drops hit and disappeared. I only had a little clearing to see where we were headed. The pack was drenched. Each pup prepared their bikes in different ways to protect their valuables from the rain. A few of the pups had waterproof panty-ears, while others covered their gear with specially made rain covers, and Cub and Megan covered up with trash bags. The rain was forcasted to be pounding us for the next couple of days - and it did.

We were told this was the land of many lakes, but I didn't see one the entire day, even though I could smell them as we passed. Megan and I stayed in the back and let Cub try to guide us to temporary protections. The pack's morale was still high on this day, but slowly it was washed away with the rain. It was funny, because we decided to eat out so we could stay inside. Luckily, no one had a problem with letting me inside. At every Mom and Pop restaurant, we were greeted with smiles and helpful hands. I'm pretty sure we ate more than we paid for at most of the places. Cub was good at finding nice places for the group to dry off, even politely asking people where we could stay for cheap. The most common replies were, "Where are you going?" And the conversations would usually suggest a nice place, but after mental debates, would usually end up with "How 'bout you stay at our place for the night. We have room." Luckily, all of our hunches about who to talk to worked to our advantage, because there are many other circumstances that would be very bad for us to be involved in. I've seen the news, I know what could happen.

This was our fourth night staying with someone different. Places are flooded in surrounding areas. The rain had been torrential. As we rode, I would hide my head behind Megan's helmet hoping it would stop the pelting. I don't think I've been completely dry since Freaky Cold Movie Town. Even things that are called waterproof weren't even close to being dry. Our pace had been slower and everyone had to avoid the big puddles that could bog us down. No one had wrecked, so it hadn't been all that bad. Without the rain we would have never met Crazy Folk singer, Charlie's Angel mayor, or Grandma Harley who we are staying with now.

Its been interesting seeing the young pups be so polite and cordial everywhere we'd stayed. They aren't that way to each other during the daytime grinds from place to place. Inside they were all different, but still the same. Alpha Jr. always volunteered to cook. I think he was trying to show off in front of Socks, because there was a grin to his volunteering that suggested some other motive. Young Pup, Slow Poke and Frenchy were now the crew. Since our record miles day, the three of them have worked well together during the day and had entertained themselves without incident, while Yeah Food and Smelly Hands were off and on toward each other. I noticed that sometimes being right next to someone all the time wasn't the best thing for either person. The quiet times Yeah Food had earlier on the trip are gone. I think she missed some of that time. How do you tell someone that you want space to yourself without hurting their feelings? It seems to me humans don't do this too well.

That's it? I don't get more? You gave Slow Poke more than me. I stand up next to Cub and reach out and lightly hit Cub on the face. He looks at me and says, "What do you want?" He knows what I want. He has another cookie in his hand and its not chocolate. I could eat it. Wait whose hand is this? Yes, Grandma Harley to the rescue.

Chapter 17

July 26th

Everywhere I look, I see things out and about. Birds are flying overhead while little rodents are playing Frogger. It's been a while since I could actually see with all of the different types of moisture: dense fog, light rain, scattered showers, and downpours. These Doggles aren't too bad. Everything looks a lot more clear now and I don't have to squint to see as we speed along. In front of us, I can see Smelly Hand's face, wait, I can actually see her face. I don't remember if I could ever see her face that clearly. She has a big smile and takes a hand off the handlebars and gives us a wave. She's probably a telephone pole away and I can still see her face. We get to the top of the little rise and I tuck my head over to the right of Megan's head. We start to move faster down the other side of the rise; I push my head farther forward to get more of the smells that are surrounding us. I can keep my eyes open even though we are cutting through the wind at a higher speed. Maybe there is an upside to these Doggles.

Today has been filled with little ups and downs, but only with the grades on the road itself. The smiles had come back with the sun itself. The rain is now out of sight and boy are we relieved. We left Grandma Harley's house early, after eating our weight in fresh baked blueberry muffins. Today, the group has no worries. We knew where we were staying that night, which is usually one of the most stressful parts of the day. The company Cub and Megan worked for had been heading cross-country for quite a few years now and over time some groups have developed continuing friendships with the individuals they had met. Tonights stay was at a couple's house that have welcomed our groups for the past four years. They were bikers in their own right, apparently. In the notes we received from the boss, it said that he races mountain bikes and road bikes. Plus, both of them have ridden across the country a couple of times. Everyone was looking forward to the guarantee of shelter for the night.

The roads had been the biggest issue of the day. The directions we had were not the best and all of the roads were labeled with one or two alphabetical letters like K or BB. Some of the pack wanted to see if we could spell words with the street names on our trip across the state, but that was quickly nixed. One of the roads we were supposed to take was completely closed due to construction. Without a current map of the state, we were at the will of the people we asked. Cub always asked more than one person to hear their options, but this time we had three people with three totally different unsure directions. And we were off. I only rode with Cub for a short section before lunch and the rest of the day I was with Megan. The strangest part of the day was that all of the male pups were hanging out all together and all the female pups were together. There hadn't been any days that I could remember there being such a division. No arguments, side comments, or even rolling eyes, the day just went smoothly within the groups. The guys took turns racing to city limit signs or various telephone poles or mailboxes. The girls tried to take pictures while riding. Those should be interesting. The poses they made will make the photos even more enjoyable.

The highlight for the entire group was lunch in a small town. There wasn't much to the town, but they did have an old light colored wood store with a porch and benches out front. Megan told the group to get what ever they wanted to eat and the pack was off for the hunt. The owner of the store let me in and introduced me to his loyal friend. His big dark buddy was deaf and going blind. He was very nice and used many gestures to show me that he would share his food and water with me. Sometimes it was nice to meet individuals who were like me. I pulled on the elder's short nub of a tail to have him come outside with the pack to see what they were eating, and he followed. Everyone in the pack introduced themselves to the elder statesman and we all just ate and then napped in the sun on the porch.

The pack is all cheers. We just passed a sign that said we were only a couple of miles from our destination. The group now rejoined into one harmonious pack. I stayed in the very back with Megan, but everyone else rotated at the front for four telephone poles then drifted right in front of us. Looking over to the right, then the left, the rows of corn are flying by. If I look at an angle, it kind of makes me a little motion sick. Keep my eyes to the front. Keep my eyes to the front. A car pulls up to the side of Megan and me. I look over and there are 3 juvenile pups looking over with big smiles. The person closest to the window yells out, "Where are you heading?".

Megan looks over and says, "Tonight, just up here, but eventually to the Atlantic Ocean."

The driver in disbelief says, "the Atlantic Ocean?"

Megan nods. They then speed up passing the group whooping and hollering and giving us thumbs up. The smiles are all around.

Chapter 18

July 27ᵗʰ

Wait....wait...wait...I was trying to tell Megan to wait for me, but she keeps pedaling the Harley look-a-like children's bike. I'm galloping right behind her back tire. I move to the left a bit then to the right to avoid her sometimes erratic steering. Cub and Yeah Food are laughing it up. Megan looks back at them...aaaahhhhh! Stop! I'm skidding right towards the falling bike. Alpha Jr. and Socks just passed in front of us on their tricycles. That was close. Oh no. I hear balls being dribbled. Its getting louder. Where's Cub? There he is. I sprint over to him and quickly meerkat. Whoo...he picks me up and calmly scratches behind my ears. I want to tell him to keep the basketballs away from me, but the dribbling has temporarily stopped.

Today had been hit and miss. By that, I mean we were hit by torrential rain and then missed any real chance of getting

94

many miles for the day. The pack was super motivated to get on their bikes after all the great stories we heard last night about cycling from our cordial hosts. There weren't many days that everyone was hyped and not distracted by one thing or another. The reality was that we got on the bikes just fine, but our journey came to a halt when darkness came about eight hours too early. Luckily, we pulled into a town just in time. We hurriedly asked for directions to any safe haven and were directed to the local library. Cub and I hung out under the large overhang that surrounded the nice sized brick building. This was the largest library the group has been to so far this trip. Everyone had their chance to e-mail their family and friends, then had plenty of time to relax, catching up on all of the magazine gossip they could. Cub waited to hear some results from the Tour day France from Megan, who was checking on the internet inside. Meanwhile, he just closed his eyes while laying his head on our backpack. I was pretty content just relaxing and getting my belly rubbed, rather than looking like a drenched rat again.

Slowly but surely, most of the pups came out to see if we could get going. You could tell that most of them realized that they wanted to get on their bikes despite the rain. Watching them come out, I could tell that Alpha Jr. and Socks joked with each other quite a bit, Yeah Food and Smelly Hands spatial concerns were temporarily at ease, and Frenchy, Slow Poke and Young Pup hung out like the best of friends. When Megan came out I went to hang with her, while Cub headed in to check the weather on-line. The thunder and lightning slowly drifted out of my reach. Cub came back out and relieved the group with simple words, "Let's go." The parade began through the town as Cub yelled out, "We have at least ten minutes before it should rain again." He then giggled as everyone gave him evil looks. We still needed to buy groceries and eat some sort of meal before we left town. The pack cruised over to one of those huge grocery and department stores that have endless isles of stuff. A manager of the store saw us pull in right as the sky released its fury with a loud crack of thunder. He asked us the norm, "Where are you headed?" And he proceeded to let us bring in all of the bikes. He let me in too. Outside the rain appeared to be headed back to the sky after it bounced off the flooded sections of the parking lot. Meanwhile inside, the store had a small pizza place for us to eat. We all tried to fill up with the buy one get one free deals.

We've been in here for a couple of hours. There is hardly anyone else in the store, so the pack has taken over its new territory, curiously checking out their surroundings. Cub puts me back down as Slow Poke throws a football his way. Megan

jumps back on the Harley and is having relay races with most of the pups. She's pulling up to Smelly Hands and without slowing down uses one of her cyclocross dismounts, putting her weight on her left pedal while swinging her right leg around behind the seat. She then places her right foot down behind her left foot on the slippery floor as she hands the handlebars over to Smelly Hands. Smelly Hands jumps on the bike...oh... her foot misses the pedal and it looks like she's going down. Yeah, she saves it, but has lost her lead to Yeah Food. We'll never leave this place. Wait, someone just dropped a pepperoni.

Chapter 19

July 29th

Let's go this way. Come on. This way, this way, this way.
Darkness surrounds us as we search frantically. I can't even see
the signposts, let alone the actual names on the sign. Seriously,
let's just sleep here in this yard. Alpha Jr. calls out, "I think its
over here." Socks tells him to be quiet in a not-so-nice way,
while most of the pups have laid their bikes on the ground with
disgust.

"We've been looking for hours. Let's just sleep here,"
Yeah Food suggests. Finally, someone's listening to me.

Tensions had risen. Since taking over the mini-mall, the
pack had been on the edge. That night, when the rains stopped,
we rode as far as we could before dark, however, this left us
without a real place to stay for the night. Eventually, we found a
church yard that look sufficient for a night's sleep. It seemed
perfect...until the morning. The grasses we were in were covered

by small blood-sucking insects...ticks. I was woken up by a shrill coming from one of the girls tents. Socks had found one in her hair, then Yeah Food found some in her sleeping bag, and so did Smelly Hands. The girls weren't very happy. Then Alpha Jr. thought it would be funny to go behind Socks and tell her there was a tick buried behind her ear, which wasn't true, but that ignited the fire. Socks went after Alpha Jr. and then Young Pup began to laugh. The laughter set off Smelly Hands and civil war had begun. Cub had gone to the closest town to surprise the group with breakfast, but even his treats for peace campaign was blown apart. Megan tried to work her magic, but the tactics that previously worked were disengaged. Instead, she served as the wall between the divided forces. I don't like yelling, so I hid in our den, hoping that a peace treaty would soon follow.

That day was the quietest ride so far. All the parties involved were grudgingly holding their own silence. Megan and I enjoyed the peaceful sounds of the ride, which was kind of ironic. We would cruise around the group to check up on everyone, but not many of the pups were willing to talk out the issues.

I could tell who we were going past based on the sounds of their bicycle wheels. Cub's and Megan's had a ratcheting sound when they quit pedaling, Slow Poke's seem to grind,

Young Pup's had a high pitched whistle, and Yeah Food's had the motorcycle effect because of the postcard from her brother she taped to her rack that hit each spoke as they turned. It was interesting to try to pick all of the sounds out with my eyes closed. It was its own little symphony with a little improvisation every now and then.

We did learn something important the past two days: if we told one sub sandwich chain that the other one gave us ten foot long subs for twenty dollars, the other restaurant would match it or beat it. We then proceeded to eat sub sandwiches for the next four meals. Our luck at finding places to stay stressed out some of the pups. Even Frenchy said it would be nice to know where we were going to stay instead of hoping the locals would hook us up with mid-western hospitality. I don't think those were his words, but that's what he meant. Tonight, Cub had used some of the companies previous trips notes to set up a place for the night. An elderly retired lady who was previously an author was more than willing to have us stop by her place for the night. She confirmed the directions were correct, and the pack was temporarily content. That wouldn't last long.

It's been a couple of hours of searching in the lakeside communities, but we haven't seen any road names that even

remotely look like the roads we need. Cub told us all to sit where I wanted to stop, and he took off a few minutes ago. We are all just sitting here. Words were like mountain lions, we know they exist, but actually hearing one was almost impossible. I have my head on Megan's leg. If we sit here long enough in this silence, everyone will be asleep. I'm still hungry, but I'm pretty sure I could sleep out the night. Here comes Cub. He's hopping and skipping, as only Cub does and he tells us that there is a house just a block away that is willing to let us sleep in their backyard.

"They also said we could use their pool," he says. I'm pretty sure I saw a couple of smiles popping through the cracks, but each pack member was trying not to show their weaknesses. This means when we get in the yard and Cub sets up the den, I can go to sleep. Hopefully, the pups can swim and sleep their problems away.

Chapter 20

July 30th

No. No. No. I try to grab onto the small doorway, but Megan moves my arms and legs away from the edge. The metal linked door is shut behind me. NO! I cower down in the corner of the small squared living quarters. "It's only for a couple of hours Gu," she states, "we'll be right over here." Wait. Wait. I could hide in your backpack. Wait. She's out of sight. I stand up and walk around in circles trying to find a comfortable spot. Cub left his sweatshirt in here for me to keep warm. It smells just like him. I lay down again. That's better. I should clean up before I go to sleep.

The heat fell upon us today. After last night's pool break, we only had a short jaunt over to this Animal Ferry. We took our time and even had the chance to hang out in a bike shop before we left the bigger city. In the shop, we tried to outlast the heat. The bicycle shop ordered us pizzas and soda, while we lounged in their air-conditioned shop watching highlights of this years Tour day France. One of the younger employees seemed to like having the female pups in the store and demonstrated his superior bike handling skills in the shop. Most of the guys were content lying on the floor watching the tube and waiting for the pizza. I was let free to roam, which doesn't happen very often. I did find a nice spot near the window where the sunlight beamed down on me, but I would still be cooled by the indoor air conditioning. Perfect. This was the life...bikes, food, sunlight, magic air, and the people that take care of me.

After cooling off for the afternoon, we took off to the ferry. It should have been short and sweet, but a few wrong turns made the trip a rush. Luckily, we still made it in plenty of time. A nice casual restaurant near the docks delivered us our evening meal before the jaunt across the lake.

I open my eyes as I notice the morning light is just starting to move away the deep darkness. There's Cub. Cub. Cub. Cub. Yes, Megan's right behind him. I can't control my excitement. The door is opening slowly, and I jolt out. Hugs and kisses for everyone. The night seemed like a week, but its time to continue the journey. Atlantic here we come.

Chapter 21

August 3rd

> *"Do you want a ride?" the gentleman asks Cub.*
>
> *"No, I want to ride," Cub replies.*
>
> *"Could I help in any way? I'm watching my four boys and they saw you and your group and were all excited about watching the bikes," the man with glasses says, "Could I carry your groceries? You could just draft behind the car to catch back with your group."*
>
> *Cub smiles as though the man said the magic words. Looks like a go.*

Four days of heat with no relief in sight. I can smell the heat in all directions. Our rides had been shorter than planned, to avoid the mid-day temperatures. Everywhere we go, people asked, "You're riding, even when its over 100?" The temperatures were out of our control and luckily, everyone knew that, but we still are going to have a tough time getting to the ocean by August 16th. The riding began just before sunrise and usually took a siesta from lunch until after dinner. It was just too hot. Some of the pups melted in the heat of the day. Head and stomach aches, cramps and dry mouths were all treated with cool water and snacks with some things called electrolytes. Anything that could help was used. Shade was our friend.

Other friends showed up throughout the four days, willing to help in a moment's notice. People drove ahead of us and had cookies and water waiting for our pleasure. They would invite us into their stores to cool off for as long as we needed. Some of the people would call friends or family ahead of us on our route to let them know we were coming. We couldn't ask for more. For all of the treasures we received, we would usually only have to say "thanks" and pose for a picture, but we could all easily manage that. All of the welcoming parties changed the packs mentality again, bringing them around to downright friendly. Thankfully.

The trials and tribulations of the pack continued. Luckily, the past four days had been filled with better times despite issues that tested their endurance and patience. The pack morale was pretty good despite the heat. Alpha Jr. and Socks have seemed to let the silliness of their fight be forgiven and forgotten. Frenchy admired all of the people who seemed to come out of nowhere to help us out. Smelly Hands and Yeah Food documented all of our new found friends taking names so that they can label the pictures they took along the trip. Young Pup and Slow Poke were devilish at times, but were, for the most part, a big part of the happy traveling pack. Cub's Feet of Death have healed miraculously with the simple use of socks and Megan has hope for the people of the country and sure is happy to tell us daily.

We are flying. Cub has positioned the bike two feet off of the station wagon's bumper. We can see through the back window the four young boys sticking their heads against the window making some interesting faces and we can see the father raising his thumb up and down. Cub takes his left hand off the bike and gives the dad a thumbs up. With the blinkers flashing on the car, and us traveling right behind it, the people and cars along the side of the road were all stares. Cub is pushing the biggest gear he has and is starting to reach his limits. He sticks out his hand level to the ground and the driver smiles and remains at that constant speed. I don't like the gassy smells, but at this speed we get to collect four times more smells than we usually get. My ears are blown back as I try to get a better look over Cub's right shoulder. Sweat drips on me. Cub is dripping from all directions. His pedal stroke is getting more uneven. The right leg smooths through the complete stroke, while the left seems to force the pedal down with a little jerk. I can tell he's trying to even out the strokes, but I think this is the hardest he's ridden since the longest day. The boys are crazy inside the car, jumping around, smiling, waving, eating burgers and boogers, but they seem to be enjoying the ride as much as we are. The driver points up ahead. There is the pack sitting in the shade, probably waiting for us to catch up after our quick snack stop. Cub waves his hand to continue forward. We pass the group and Cub screams. The pack looks at us and the smiles are huge. Cub makes a stop sign to the dad and we pull off to the right of the car. That was fun.

Chapter 22

August 4th

    We've just left the country. The paperwork is done and we are off to see the land of the maple leaves. Megan and I are following the pack along a walkway. It doesn't smell any different than the States. We are just smoothly moving along: sun drifting down, no wind, and no problems. Smelly Hands and Slow Poke are just in front of us, maybe 6 or 7 bike lengths. We can see Cub at the front of the pack with Yeah Food and Young Pup directly behind. They cross the busy road and then wait at the corner for the rest of us. We have to cross a set of railroad tracks then wait for the traffic signal to change. Smelly Hands moves in front of Slow Poke as the walkway narrows before the tracks. Oh no! Smelly Hands hit the tracks and her front wheel fell right into the track grooves! The next thing I know, she's on the ground. She didn't have time to hit the brakes. As her bike stopped, she flew right over the bars landing partially on grass and the tracks. Oh no. Oh no. Slow Poke is just too close. He

can't avoid the bike barrier! He propels himself off the bike and the organized pieces of metal collided together. He landed shoulder first onto the ground. So much for no problems.

Our day had been going so smoothly. We started before the heat and sped along to the border. All of the pups were motivated to get to a place where they could buy some sort of souvenirs for friends, family and themselves. We had plenty of time to check out all the cheesy shops as the pack could. Cub looked for a cheap pair of sunglasses since he'd lost two pairs already on the trip. Most of the young ones searched frantically for a flag to place on the back of their gear to support the new country ahead. Yeah Food took time to call home on a pay phone while all the other pups were more than content spending money. They were running out of days to take advantage of this luxury fund their parents alloted for souvenirs.

After an afternoon of shopping, eating and relaxing, we were off to cross the bridge into a new world. The bridge itself was the most interesting part of the day for me. They waited until all was clear then the uniformed humans escorted us across the bridge by following us with one of their fancy lighted cars. They warned us of the grooves that were similar to the railroad track grooves. These grooves had taken down many a cyclist.

Our pack made it without incident. All that was left was to clear the paperwork with the border patrol and we would be off for the evening jaunt. Apparently, my paperwork was the most confusing. It took a little time out of our waning sunlight. I had given my cute face to the guard and then we were through.

A man with dark, nicely groomed hair was sitting next to the fallen victims. He had seen the accident from his car and pulled over to help us out. He's a physician at the local hospital. He asks Smelly Hands a few questions and she responds without hesitation. The man continues to ask questions while scanning over the carnage, or lack of it.

The group is starting to get antsy with the sunlight drifting out of sight. Megan and I are hanging with the rest of the pups while Cub and the Doctor continue to talk. Cub has a big smile as he walks away from the Doctor.

"Hey, at least we now have a place to stay," he says "They will be fine after some icing and ibuprofen." Faces of nervous energy were now replaced with gentle smiles.

Chapter 23

August 7ᵗʰ

I hate traffic. AHH! That was close. Young Pup, stay to the right. Megan yells out, "To the right." Traffic is flying by us, sometimes only leaving a couple of inches for us to ride. The shoulder of the road is lacking and its not the best time of day to be riding through this part of town. Rush hour. I hate it. The pack is almost in a straight line with little space between each of us. We just want to get to our hotel for the night. It can't be much longer. BEEP...BEEEEEEPPP. That person wasn't happy with us. Sometimes the honks are from the happy people, but not right now.

Dr. Dreamy turned out to be a favorite among the ladies. Smelly Hands loved the attention while Socks and Yeah Food hoped for an injury that needed his care. Smelly Hands was pretty sore from the accident, but luckily, she didn't break her collarbone or anything of that sort. She had road rash and a little bruising, while Slow Poke was just sore, but both were told to take a day off, Doctor's orders. So a day off we had. This town was interesting and Cub kept referring to it as the Chronicles. I didn't get it, but I rarely got his references. The day off was nice, but in the back of everyone's minds we knew that these days off meant more time on the bike later.

The good Doctor had plenty of room at his house on the outskirts of town. He was a great host, buying enough food for a country and allowing the pack to use his television and computer. We couldn't ask for much more. The day off was a serious day off. No one wanted to do anything except lounge around. The Doctor took a day off from work to escort us to some of the local highlights, but quickly noticed the group didn't need much to be satisfied.

Socks and Alpha Jr. happily enjoyed each other's company. Smelly Hands was content laying around with minimal movement, while Slow Poke stared intently at the television almost as if it was new to him. Young Pup tried to instigate the others, but no one seemed to care. Megan tried to translate all of the things labeled in French, but Frenchy was better at it for some reason. With all of them entertaining themselves, Cub and I worked on some of the bikes and ate junk food. I'm better at the latter.

After the day off at the Chronicles, heat continued to dominate the weather, with no end in sight. The time on the bike was long and hot. The first major town we hit had a water park. The park was on the outer parts of the town, but with many directions from the locals we finally made it. Cub and I sat outside, since Cub can't swim, but all of the others were ecstatic about the chance to cool off. We napped in the shade and awoke from drips of cold water and Megan giggling while looking down at us.

Cooling off was the focus. There were times when Cub was in the back because Megan wasn't feeling well. Cub liked the heat, and also likes to be able to make sure the rest of the pack is safe. We stayed as a uniform pack, always riding within sight of each other. The day after the water park, we struggled pedaling our bikes in the heat of the day, but the group wanted their day off at the upcoming Famous Falls, so we pushed on. Finally, after riding hours in the heat, Cub had everyone pull off the road. There weren't any cool places to hang out throughout the day, but Cub knew we all needed a break. He walked into this bar just off the side of the road, since there was no other businesses in sight, and asked if all of us could come in. I was surprised, with me on Cub's back, that the bearded fellow didn't hesitate in welcoming us into his sports bar. He was a pretty big fellow, taller than Slow Poke, with the enjoyment of food filling out his face and belly. My eyes took time to adjust to the dark room, but once they did they started to focus on the food that was in front our group.

"What do you want?" he asked Cub. I wanted the chicken strips and Cub must have been listening, because he ordered chicken strips, fries, and soda all around.

Along with the comfort foods, the locals here were more than comfortable with us in the bar. They asked all the normal questions, with one exception, "Are we nicer than people you've come across so far?"

Alpha Jr. came back with a quick response, "We'll wait till the end of the trip and we'll drop ya a note to let you know."

I gotta go pee. No more pictures. We're posing here for some of the tourists, but our novelty is spreading like a wildfire. Pictures, pictures and more pictures. The pack is pushing their bikes across the cross walk and this looks like the place. Finally we're here. Cub puts me down. Whew. Ah, nice soft grass. AH. I roll around scratching my back. This is great. Okay. Pick me up, too many people.

Chapter 24

August 11th

Do I look bigger? I feel a bit heavy, but do I look bigger? The pack is spread out over the entire front of the grocery store temporarily delaying getting back on the bikes. No one is paying attention to me. I prance around trying to get their attention, occasionally stopping in front of the different pup, wondering if they think I'm gaining weight or not. I prance around some more and finally Yeah Food, Smelly Hands and Slow Poke look over to me. Quickly, I meerkat to show them my belly. Okay, tell me if I look big or not. "Gu, you're cute," Yeah Food says. Well, that doesn't answer my question, but at least I still look cute.

Days off have been good to us until now. Everyone loved the time spent at the actual Falls itself, but our last day off had turned into a soap opera, with drama everywhere. Everyone wanted to do something, but everyone's something was different. A few pups eventually went to the movies while the others cruised through all of the touristy shops. The tensions that have come and gone all came back at the highest level. Young Pup said something that put him in the dog house and Frenchy finally let his feelings be known. Finally, I can understand every word that comes out of his mouth, but many of the words on our day off were not happy ones. He felt some of the pups in the group had gotten their way for most of the trip and he was tired of their whining. This, of course, didn't go over well with the pack, even if it was true. Our day off ended with a long, drawn out discussion. I fell asleep a couple of times, but it continued on without a say from me. No one looked happy at the end of the discussion, but it appeared most of the pups spoke their mind and were ready to go to bed.

At the Famous Falls, Cub and Megan worked out the math and determined that the pack would have to average close to eighty miles a day over the next eight days to get to the Ocean on time. They tried to round up on the miles, because by bike we can't go the most direct route that the gassers could go. Eight days of riding will seem like 56 days to me, but it will go by quick for everyone else. After all of the day off negativity, our next day didn't start in the best way either. A Mounty, a fancy dressed police officer, told us that a cyclist was killed by a gasser a couple of days ago as he left the Famous Falls. When we jumped back on our bikes, we remembered quickly the horrid traffic that we ran into two days ago. Once we drifted away from the Famous Falls, the traffic continued, but the pack held their lines and followed the traffic rules for bikes. The traffic would come and go, but nothing was as bad as rush hour to the Famous Falls. We have had thousands of gassers pass us with only five or so giving us any problems, but most humans remember those five gassers rather than all of those vehicles that slowed down, moved over, or even cheered us on on our journey. That's unfortunate.

On the second day we had to rush into Other Falls in order to get the mail before the post office closed. Some of the pack's bikes were not in that much of a hurry, deciding to release the air out of a few tires making them flat as pancakes. Finally, Cub and I were willing to take on the next mission for the group. We took off ahead of the pack to try to get to Other Falls before five when the post office would close. I would stick my head behind Cub's head as he went down to the drops to battle through the segments with a slight headwind. The roads were a little up and down. There were no mountains or challenging pitches, but still a little more enjoyable than the miles of straight, flat roads we'd encountered on the trip. Every once in a while I would stick my head to his right side to see our path in front of us. The wide roads and shoulders were ideal for our high speed chase. The time trial took its toll on Cub though. The pace that he maintained earlier on the course couldn't be kept as we closed in on Other Falls. He would stand up to try to find some more strength, but he had to back down a little in order to even finish the trial he had started. When we pulled into the town, his strength had temporarily come back. The post office's doors were closed. Cub then put his head down. It was before five, but the post office had closed at four-thirty. We then walked around the brick building and we heard, "Cute dog." One of the uniformed carriers was sitting in back of the building getting ready to leave. To make things short, we picked up our last mail drop, but it was close. Whew.

118

While we ate pizza, the pack enjoyed their last care packages on the trip. They then realized we were almost done. Almost all of the negative feelings were packed away in the care packages - hopefully packed away for good.

Last night's sleep was the most peaceful sleep I've had in days. We've just left a touristy village next to a lake. It was a beautiful place. Trees, water, humans exercising, relaxing, and walking with my kind on a clear, crisp sunny day. We're back on our bikes and everyone has ice cream. Cub hates cones, because he likes the melty stuff, but on the bike a cone will have to do. I'm on his right shoulder. I can almost reach it. It's melting...let me have some. I can help. I can help. He's holding a straight line, but more of the ice cream is flying past my head than is going in his or my mouth. It's like catching flies by tongue. Yeeahh. He's holding the handlebar with his right hand and reaches over with his left hand. ICE CREAM. Ohh...vanilla. It's all over my face and I can't reach half of it. I'm looking to the left. There's a car with some pretty old humans. Great...their gonna take a picture of me with ice cream all over my face.

Chapter 25

August 13th

You can take him. Get on his wheel. Quick, get on his wheel. Cub pulls up behind Frenchy's wheel. He stands for a few strokes then sits back down. Frenchy looks back. "You can lead," he says. Cub just shakes his head from side-to-side. Frenchy gives a quirky smile and increases his pace. Cub stands to hold his ground behind him. Looking to the left, it looks like we are above the stormy farmlands. Dark puffy clouds fill the sky to our left, but to our right we have light thin clouds. We hit the top of the hill and Cub stands and with all the muscles on his arms and legs, pushes the bike as fast as he can. The draft pulls us up to Frenchy and then propels us past him. Frenchy yells, "No passing on downhills, you said." Cub's smile gets as big as any I've ever seen.

We've had to conquer the hills the past couple of days, but also were able to enjoy some nice relaxed riding past beautiful rolling vistas. The hills after the lake were bigger than we expected, but everyone seemed to be on a new riding skills level. All of those pups who struggled on the mountains early on the journey were keeping pace and even passing some of the pups who previously excelled. The comfort and improvement was shown on one hill in particular. Entering the City of Orange Men, we had to conquer those uphills, but enjoyed pushing our bikes and nerves to the edge on the downhills. The last downhill was most epic. Cub led the pack down and it was fast. It wasn't very long, but the speeds were faster than anything we had hit before. The best part was that after the speed dramatically increased, there was a depression on the road that made me lose my stomach. When Megan reached the rest of us, everyone quickly scrolled through their features on their cyclometer to see what their max speed was. 49.7, 48.9, and 49.6 were all yelled out, but no one was slower than 48 miles an hour. Their confidence was obvious when a few of the pups wanted to ride back up the hill, just to come down again. Unfortunately, time was against us.

Since we've passed the Famous Falls, everyone we spoke with about cycling informed us of a set of trails that followed some old canals. Due to the mail drop, we couldn't follow the earlier trails, but out of the City of Orange Men, we had our first look at the trail system. It took some time to find the entry to the trail, but once on it, we had no worries. Made out of broken rocks of some sort, the trail was easily accessible by our bikes without knobs. We knew we could stay on this trail until it ended, passing old towns that were built because of the canals. Without gas traffic, our stresses were eased, but our pace was slower on the trail. All of the people we passed were excited to see our group and were willing to offer us advice or directions. It was slow, but a nice break from the roads we'd ridden the rest of the day.

Frenchy pulls up to our back wheel. I look at him. He

smiles. Stroke for stroke, up the hill. Cub surges and looks around. Frenchy's right there. Cub surges again. A little gap, nope, he's back on our wheel. We summit the hill and Cub relaxes with a few soft pedal strokes. Frenchy jumps...pushing his biggest gear as quick as he can. He has a gap. Cub didn't react quick enough, but he pounds on the pedals. We're in our most aero position. Cub's chin is almost touching the stem. I get my head down and try to lie my ears down, but they sometimes have a mind of their own. We got him. Cub sits up a bit as we close in on Frenchy. We'll take him on the next hill. We pull to Frenchy's left side and he says, "Winner top of next hill." Cub nods up-and-down.

Chapter 26

August 15th

I can't keep my eyes open. Are we there yet? We haven't taken a long break all day. I get off to pee and get a snack and we're back on the bike. Megan reaches her hand toward me, "We're almost there." She puts her hand back on the handlebar and continues to spin the pedals. She's spinning more than powering through the stroke, trying to conserve her energy, the little she has left. We both look back to see how the young pups are fairing. They are all within sight. I can even see Cub way in the distance talking to Young Pup.

While the miles have been ticking down, the humans we meet on the trip have continued to amaze the young pups. The past two nights we'd been welcomed into people's yards before we could even ask where to find a good cheap place to stay. Yesterday, we passed the big city of She's Next To Me, and were given directions by a pizza delivery boy who was generous enough to bring us some pizza down the road. While riding, we merged with a group of cyclists who were out for an evening ride. When they started to pass us, they giggled when they saw Megan and I, so they slowed down to ask us where we were headed. We were all heading the same general direction and that was how we found our place of rest for the night. All we had to do was follow their lead to the gentleman's house.

I noticed the group was a perfect display of teamwork. They weren't all racing cyclists, but some were, while others were just out for the enjoyment of the ride. Others were in the group to help them get their exercise to improve their health, but all of them worked together like a flock of geese migrating for the season. The pulls up front were nice and smooth, no accelerations or jerky steering. All of their outfits were different, but each individual had their own matching jersey and shorts. I'm glad I'm color blind, because I can't imagine the montages that were created with those designs. Our pack tried to work in the group, but it was obvious that our skill level was years behind theirs. Despite their experience, the group was willing to let us try and learn some of their skills. It didn't take long to cover the last twenty miles of the day, and we quickly arrived at our rest stop for the evening. After looking at all the pups' faces, you could tell that although the group ride made most of them a little nervous, it also made the miles fly by without much thought.

After waving goodbye to our hosts the next morning, we all knew what was in store for today. In past years with this touring company, the pack would eat a fancy dinner after they arrived at the Ocean, but this year it had to change. Frenchy's flight was taking off late tomorrow, but that would mean that he would miss the final dinner. The pack decided to have the final dinner today, the last full day together. Unfortunately, this meant that we would have to ride over 110 miles through the roughest terrain we've had since Going to the Sun. A hundred miles on flat land was tough enough, but now, over mountains, we needed to add at least ten more miles to that total. We also had to be done before 7pm to meet our reservation for dinner in the Grape

Plane city. That was a challenge.

Our departure in the morning was at the first sign of light. We had breakfast after riding for 2 hours at 7:40 am. The towns we cruised through today had a different feel than many of those we've stopped by on our journey. The smells were different. We didn't get to spend much time in the coffee smelling old brick building towns, but the general atmosphere has changed. Our journeys into the lush treed mountains, were a pleasant change. Traveling miles, without seeing a building makes the journey even more exciting. Now the climbs were not short and steep, but long and gradual. No one seemed to hurt on the climbs either. We had to slow, of course, but the pack was now a strong confident group that knew they could conquer these mountains. Pedaling, pedaling, and pedaling some more. I rode with Cub early in the day, but switched off to Megan once the major mountains had passed.

Out of the mountains, we cruised through small towns left and right, each with their own little niche in history. We took our last break at four o'clock, and we knew that our pace could not wane over the last 45 miles. Fifteen miles an hour. We had no choice.

Our hotel. YEAH. We're here. Let me out. Megan

disconnects me from my seat. I pee...no sniffing right now, I have to go. The pups are slowly pulling in. Slow Poke, Smelly Hands, Yeah Food, Socks, Alpha Jr., Young Pup and Cub. We made it. Surprisingly, I'm not hungry. I just want to go to bed. Cub picks me up. Good night.

Chapter 27

August 16th

"You're almost there," a lady calls out from her passing car. She must be one of the young pup's family. At least six cars have passed us to cheer us on then would drive further up the road to cheer again. Megan and I are leading the pack to the final frontier, trying to slow their thirst to sprint on by with an early attack on the prey. Megan knows that we need to save enough energy to finish off the hunt. We are flying compared to most of the trip, trees are whipping by us at an alarming, but constant rate. I can smell the Ocean. I can smell the Ocean. We are all ready to pounce.

After the longest pack ride of the trip, we all enjoyed our last dinner together. Everyone showered in their rooms and put on the nicest clean clothes they had left. We ate at an Italian eatery that had outdoor seating, mostly for my convenience. It was great. Each person ate whatever they wanted on the menu and I even was given my own plate with mini meatballs. The food was delicious and the pack graced tired smiles. We ate till our bellies were content.

When dinner ended, we sat around the large round table and had our final discussion. It was an open discussion about anything, but it quickly turned into the highlights of the trip. I listened to their discussion, but as I looked around at the young pups, each face now brought back memories or emotions that weren't there at the beginning of the journey.

Alpha Jr. and Socks seemed to grow on each other as the trip pedaled by. Despite a few rough spells, these two were inseparable for the second half of the journey. Alpha Jr. was as confident as ever, but would use that confidence for good purposes, rather than bad. Socks had found someone to talk to who would actually listen to her. Both of them said their favorite part of the trip was the people they met on the road and their new found friendships.

The quiet and compassionate Yeah Food broke out of her shell and became the life of the party, or at least part of the life of the party. She still enjoyed time to herself and still missed home, but she now looked comfortable with everyone in the group, even Young Pup. The soreness she had earlier in the summer eventually disappeared into strong, new muscles she was happy to show off. Her smile was genuine and is probably why she enjoyed documenting the random acts of kindness that followed us here.

Helping her document the names, Smelly Hands was great at remembering all of those little things that most of the other pups seemed to forget. She and Yeah Food will probably e-mail each other and they will continue to build their bond. Smelly Hands actually turned out to be one of the better smelling pups of the trip as she didn't partake in the longest without a shower contest. She was proud to point out that everyone easily pedaled up Going to the Sun road, and she hopes they can all do it again someday.

The biggest transformation on the trip was Slow Poke. His name didn't do him justice. He was probably the best rider out of the pack and rarely had to be waited on, at least not more than the rest of the pups. His face is slimmer and his smile even bigger. His confidence rivals that of Alpha Jr.'s, and his soft-spoken demeanor is more than one could want. He was proud to point out that he had lost 45 pounds this summer, but was proudest to say that he rode almost 150 miles in one afternoon.

Young Pup was still the hardest to trust pup, but he would sometimes show signs of stardom. Last night he made most of the pack tear up, even if some of them won't admit it. He was hesitant on telling everyone that they were the nicest and best friendships he's ever had and he was sorry if he hurt anyone's feelings when he tried to fit in. He was still young and will continue to learn not to force friendships.

As we wound down, Frenchy was ecstatic to be almost done with the journey across the United States. Everyone in the group loved talking or hanging with him and could see how comfortable he was talking in front of all of them. His simple smile made me comfortable with him, which is not very common for me to say. He put what everyone had said and thought into a simple phrase, "Best moments of life, right."

Megan and Cub both thanked the group and later talked to each person individually. The one suggestion that Alpha Jr.

wanted to make clear was for someone to write a book about this trip across the country. He had a title and everything, "Adventures of the Great Chiweenie". The pack, with their tired eyes, all had one last laugh for the night.

The trees are gone in front of us. All I see is sand and water. Megan and I get off the bike. Megan lets me free. Each of the pups arrive and throw their bikes to the side to finish off the hunt. It's a race to the Ocean. Cub is jogging in the back with me passing by a littering of shoes and helmets. The Pack had their kill. I don't want to get wet. I'll stop here. Cub pulls out the camera as all of the pups are splashing around in the

water. I'm just sitting in the sand. People that we saw earlier in the cars are running and walking toward their pups. The crowd grows around us and I'm beginning to worry I might get stepped on. I meerkat. Cub picks me up, "Best moments in life, right."

WHERE IN THE WORLD IS GU?

Try to figure out all of the places that are mentioned in this book and check out the website (www.thegreatchiweenie.com) to find out how you could win one of the jerseys I'm showing off on the last page. Listed below are the towns or cities we visited (and an occasional mountain range, pass, campground or park).

Coffee City	**Dish Soap Mountains**
Western-esque Town	**Poop Poop Pass**
Shorebird Pass	**Duck Lake**
Sandy Land	**Billy**
Going to the Sun	**Fishy Town**
Fast Food Lodge	**Baby Shampoo Campground**
Got Milk River	**College Town**
Presidential Park	**Famous Authorville**
Hawaiian Wood Campground	**Freaky Cold Movie Town**
Moopshead	**Hall-of-Famer Campground**
Animal Ferry (across which of the Great Lakes)	
Land of the Maple Leaves (nation)	
The Chronicles	**Famous Falls**
Other Falls	**City of Orange Men**
She's Next To Me	**Grape Plane City**

Look at a map. Ask a friend, parent, or relative. Remember, Cub is the one who makes up the names because he can't say things, can't remember, or just likes to be silly.

www.thegreatchiweenie.com

THANKS...

I want to thank all of the people who helped out with this project. Hannah, Casey, Ronn, and Joe for their artistic and computer advice. Liz, Ed, Amber, and Megan for their editing and proofreading. All of the people who we bounced ideas off of or just rambled to. We greatly appreciate all the help from the campers that helped as well. Adopt a pet. Keep riding. Smile.

About the author: Gu, a.k.a. "The Great Chiweenie", is a adopted dog rescued from a pound in Fresno, California. He goes on occasional mountain, road and cyclocross rides with his adopted parents and can be seen cheering on his parents at the many races in California. He doesn't like to get dressed up, but does occasionally for photo shoots. The Doggles are used to protect his eyes as recommended by his eye doctor. Cubby is just one of the parents Gu rides with who helped with this book.